One
Monday
Prayer

T.K. Chapin

One
MONDAY
PRAYER

T.K.
CHAPIN

One Monday Prayer

ISBN-13:
978-1539969761

ISBN-10:
1539969762

DEDICATION

Dedicated to my loving wife.

For all the years she has put up with me

And many more to come.

CONTENTS

ACKNOWLEDGMENTS

First and foremost, I want to thank God. God's salvation through the death, burial and resurrection of Jesus Christ gives us all the ability to have a personal relationship with the creator of the Universe.

I also want to thank my wife. She's my muse and my inspiration. A wonderful wife, an amazing mother and the best person I have ever met. She's great and has always stood by me with every decision I have made along life's way.

I'd like to thank my editors and early readers for helping me along the way. I also want to thank all of my friends and extended family for the support. It's a true blessing to have every person I know in my life.

AUTHOR'S NOTE

Thank you for choosing to read **One Monday Prayer**. I wrote this book to help people that are going through difficulties in their life. Oftentimes it's not until we stop trying that God can truly begin to work in our lives. The story centers on a widow that visits her cousin (Serenah) for the Holidays. Through a near death experience she finds comfort in a prayer of a stranger. The truth this story draws on is one near to my heart, that's God is always working behind the scenes. It also touches on healing after loss. My hope for this story is that it blesses you as much as it did me writing it.

And we know that in all things God works for the good of those who love him, who[a] have been called according to his purpose.
Romans 8:28

When we use the Scriptures as a blueprint for our life, blessings follow. God doesn't promise everything will be perfect, but He does promise to lift us up when we fall. If you need help aligning your life with the Bible, I recommend picking up a free thirty-day devotional that will be delivered to your inbox to get you jump-started. To claim, visit tkchapin.com/devotional

CHAPTER 1

At gate forty-seven in the Tampa International
Airport, I dabbed on a little frankincense oil to help
settle my nerves. The cashier at the gift shop insisted
that the oil worked great for anxiety. Unfortunately,
it wasn't working very well. The knot of anxiety in
the center of my chest tightened and expanded as I
waited for my plane.

I loathed flying almost as much as I hated the
holidays the last three years without Ted. We were
married for only two years, but each holiday was a
reminder of the life I would never have with Ted and

4

the dreams of a future we once made together.

"Zone one is now ready to board," a woman's scratchy voice said over the intercom. The knot in my chest grew in width and depth at the announcement of my zone.

Watchful eyes focused on me with looks of envy as I stood up and made my way over to the line. First class had that effect on people. While the rest were stuck with all the crying babies and seats that were packed too tightly, first class was comfortable. This wasn't my choice, but my cousin Serenah's.

She wanted me comfortable.

It took her over a year of phone calls to get me to visit her in Newport, Washington, and I think she felt bad about what helped me finally agree to come—my apartment caught fire. With a timeline of two plus weeks until the landlord could get me into a new place, I didn't see any reason why I shouldn't visit.

The line shifted a few paces.

Attempting to focus on my breathing, I was minding my own business when a man in front of me turned around. He looked at me for a second and then shifted his gaze to somewhere behind me. Then he took the liberty of looking at me again. Our eyes met for a moment, but I shifted my eyes to a row of seats nearby.

"You going to Detroit?" the man asked.

Shaking my head, I looked at him. "No. Just passing through. I connect out." Conversations, or more specifically, small talk, weren't something I was interested in. Especially with men. They had a way of taking a simple conversation and thinking I was interested. Turning my head, I looked over at the row of seats again.

I saw a child.

Not over three or four years old, the little boy was smiling as he pushed a train back and forth on the floor and made train sounds as he went. Peering up at his mother and father, I flashed them a smile. My heart longed for a family ever since I was young enough to chase my siblings around the house. Ted and I were going to have kids at the five-year mark of our marriage.

Arriving at the ticket booth, the lady took my five hundred and thirty-two-dollar piece of paper. She tore off a portion, handing only a remnant back to me.

"Thank you."

As I walked down the narrow jetway toward the plane, I prayed for safe travels for not only myself, but everyone up in the air that day.

Stepping over the small gap of space between the plane and the jetway, I noticed the runway not far below. I lifted my eyes, and they fell on two flight attendants and a pilot. They all welcomed me with smiles and handshakes that helped my anxiety a smidge. There was something about meeting the pilot that settled my nerves.

After finding my seat, I peered out the window and stared at the other planes I could see off in the distance. Some were landing, and others were getting ready to take off. So many planes and so many people, all coming and going for the holidays. Eventually, the plane filled up and I thought myself lucky since the seat beside me was empty. Then, just as the door was being shut by one of the flight attendants, a blond guy in a gray suit grabbed the door from shutting.

They let him on.

Holding my breath, I watched nervously as he chatted the flight attendants up and apologized for his lateness. He came down the aisle and our eyes connected. He glanced up at the number and then his ticket.

He sat down.

Letting the air out of my lungs, my shoulders slumped and I turned my eyes back to the window.

"Sorry to disappoint."

Turning my head, I nodded to acknowledge his comment but kept looking outside.

"I like it when there's an empty seat beside me. Makes me less nervous about flying."

Turning to him as the engines fired up, I felt like talking could distract me. "You don't like flying?" I asked.

Buckling his seat belt, he shook his head. "Hate it. I like to be on the ground. Even though planes are the safest way to travel, they freak me out."

"Me too," I replied. Watching, I saw him retrieve a pair of ear buds from his backpack and plug them into his phone. "What are you listening to?"

"It's a pretty broad mix. I really like jazz."

Nodding, I said, "Jazz is nice. I like a little bit of everything, but I *love* the violin."

My eyes shifted back to the window as the plane began rolling. My heart raced as I prayed fervently for God to keep us all safe on the flight. *Cast all your fears and anxieties on the Lord, Angie,* I thought to myself.

The plane jolted forward.

Pushing my palm against the seat in front of me, I

took notice of my breathing and started taking deep breaths. *C'mon, Angie. We haven't even taken off yet. Keep it together. Worst case scenario? You get to see Jesus today. That's a pretty good worst case scenario.* My breathing came back under my control as the flight attendants got into position to go over safety while flying.

As the woman over the intercom system talked about the seat being a life preserver, the man beside me snickered.

"What's so funny?" I inquired.

He leaned over and said, "How is that going to save us in *any* circumstance?"

Laughing a little, I caught the attention of the flight attendant. She flashed a forced and plastic smile over at me for a second and then continued with the presentation.

Successfully avoiding any additional small talk from the attractive gentleman sitting beside me on the plane, I made it to Detroit and connected to Seattle. I didn't notice, but he had also been on the flight from Detroit to Seattle. After getting off the plane in Seattle, I found my way over to The Coffee Bean and Tea Leaf, a little coffee shop inside the airport, as I waited for the flight to Spokane.

As I read an email from my landlord that came through on my phone during the last flight, I was interrupted.

"You drink coffee too?" the man from the plane asked as he walked through the trellis and into the sitting area of the coffee shop.

Peering up at him, I nodded and couldn't help but smile at the enthusiasm he held for such a rudimentary fact.

"Sure do," I replied.

Turning my eyes back to the phone to help communicate the fact that I didn't want him to come over to the table, I glanced up a moment later to see where he was now. Watching, I saw him order a coffee, but when he handed his money over to the cashier, he glanced behind him for a moment. *What is that about?* He turned his body toward me, and I jerked my eyes back to my phone to hide my interest. Slowly, I looked again. Now he was waiting at the end of the counter for his coffee. As he waited, he tapped his fingers on the countertop and kept a smile on his face. The person standing in line behind him previously walked over to him and shook his hand with a smile on her face. *Ahh, he's one of those kind of guys.*

Boarding the plane an hour later, I laughed as I found us in the exact seats we were in during our flight from Tampa to Detroit.

I smiled as I scooted past him, and he looked up at me. "I wasn't late this time."

Getting comfortable in my seat, I set my purse down at my feet and caught his eyes still on me. In an attempt to shoo his interest away from me, I brought up what I had seen earlier. "Did you have a good coffee date with that gal?"

He leaned in toward me. "What are you talking about?"

"The girl you bought coffee for earlier."

"Ooooh. That." He laughed and sat back in his seat. Glancing over at me, he leaned in. "I bought the whole line of people coffee. Not just that girl."

Taken aback, I shook my head. "Why would you do something like that?"

"Um. It's a nice thing to do? Plus, it's the season for giving." He pulled out a small candy cane from his front suit pocket and handed it to me. "I know it's a little early, but Merry Christmas."

"Yes. Five weeks away, but how sweet."

He laughed. "Literally."

A few minutes later, he put in a pair of ear buds and leaned his head back against the seat, closing his eyes.

Turning my head, I focused on the runway and prayed for another safe flight.

Not a half hour later, the flight was interrupted by a rough patch of turbulence.

The plane shook, and luggage tumbled from the overhead compartments and into the aisle.

Clutching onto both armrests, I felt my insides rumble. The pilot came over the intercom. "We're flying into some bad weather. Please make sure your seatbelt is on and you are securely in your seats."

Shaking of the plane worsened.

Then the plane dropped.

Screams erupted.

Clutching the armrests tightly as my knuckles went white, I prayed. I felt my heart pound against my ribcage and my faith falter. *Come on, get it under control. We're almost done with the flight.*

When the oxygen masks suddenly fell from the ceiling, I lost it. Tears streamed down my cheeks as I reached up and attempted to untangle the mask

from the knot of tubes.

The knotted tubes weren't coming undone.

The man beside me reached up and untangled them.

Reaching over, he placed it around my face and our

eyes met. I saw the fear in his eyes that I felt in my

heart as the lights flashed in the plane. As the plane

turned to one side and screams from others grew

louder, I just kept looking into his eyes. Suddenly, I

felt a touch as one of the man's hands found mine.

We clutched our hands together and leaned into one

another.

He began praying. His voice rattled and was muffled

by all that was going on around us, yet somehow, I

could hear him. "Father, we come to you not

knowing the outcome. Please help us in our time of

need. Please, Lord, save us." In the midst of the most

fearful moment of my life, I found myself in prayer with a stranger.

Our hands locked and we kept staring into each other's eyes in what was probably one of the most intense moments of my life. Life and death danced in the moment. Anything could happen.

Soon, the plane regained control and leveled out. It was over.

As we released our hands from one another and breathed a sigh of relief, the pilot came over the intercom and apologized. The pilot's voice sounded rattled over the circumstances we had endured. The screaming had stopped and a quiet weeping took its place in the plane.

As the plane started its descent not long after to land in Spokane, the stranger reached below his feet and opened his backpack. Pulling out a small white cardboard box, he turned to me. My eyes traced the outline of the box as he handed it to me.

Shaking my head, I looked at him. "What is this for?"

Pushing a smile, he tilted his head. The way he looked into my eyes right in that moment struck a chord inside me. Like a strum of a violin, the sound of his voice echoed through my body and a warmth radiated from inside me. "A thank you. You let me hold your hands and pray with you. That meant the world to me and more than you'll ever know." His eyes fell to the box. "My business card is in there too. Call me sometime."

CHAPTER 2

As I exited the Spokane International Airport's revolving doors, I was greeted by a gust of chilly winter air and flakes of snow. Not having ever experienced snow in Florida, I was startled by the coldness the flakes brought as they bounced against my skin. Even with all the coldness of winter, I couldn't help but still carry a sense of joy for making it to Spokane alive.

With my purse atop my suitcase and the white cardboard box tucked away inside my luggage, I strolled down the sidewalk with my head bowed in pursuit of a cab. Soon, a cab pulled up beside me, splashing through some of the slush that had

collected near the curb. The passenger side window

rolled down and a man leaned over the console.

"Hey, Miss. You need a ride?"

Lifting my eyes as I shielded the winter elements

with an arm, I nodded. "Desperately!"

"Get in!"

I went to the back door of the cab as another gust of

wind swooped in and pushed part of my pea-coat up

to one side, letting a sliver of cold wind shoot up

into my shirt. I let out a shriek. Grabbing my

suitcase and purse, I tossed them into the back and

got into the cab, slamming the door shut. My teeth

clattered as I rubbed my arms, trying to recapture

the warmth I once knew.

Laughing, the cab driver adjusted the rearview

mirror and looked at me. "Where you from?"

"Florida."

"Ah . . . Florida. Far colder here. Yes?"

"It sure is." Glancing out my window, I saw the man from the plane going into the parking garage. I felt a connection with him now, like I knew him or something. Part of me wished we would have talked more.

"Where can I take you?" the cab driver asked, breaking into my thoughts.

"Here," I replied, handing him the address to the *Inn at the Lake.*

"Beautiful lake," the driver said, putting the car into drive. "You will have a good time there."

Peering out the window of the cab, I thought about the stranger, our prayer, and our brush with death. It was surreal to me now, almost like a dream or something. He was there with me and I was there with him. The moment would stay with me always.

Arriving at the inn, I paid the cab driver and got out.
Setting my purse atop my suitcase, I grabbed onto
the handle and rolled it down the snow- and ice-
covered driveway toward the inn's front door. My
mouth gaped open at the sight of the inn and the
frozen lake that sat behind it. *Serenah has been living
here?* I thought to myself as I could hear shards of
ice break beneath my heels. Serenah had done well
for herself living with her ex-husband, John, back in
Albany, but it was always *his* house and *his* property
and *his* money, according to him and the prenuptial
agreement Serenah signed before the marriage.
A Christmas wreath hung from a nail on the front

door of the inn. When the door opened, the wreath shook, dropping a pile of snow into the entry, and there stood my cousin whom I hadn't seen in years. She glowed with a radiance that I once knew for myself. She looked happy. Never did I see the same sort of joy radiate from her in the years she was with John. Gripping tighter to the handle, I scurried the rest of the span of driveway that separated us, continuing down the rock salted stairs to her. Letting go of my suitcase, I wrapped my arms around her and let the warmth of her hug sweep over me.

The warmth of familiarity coursed through my body as we embraced. It had been five years since we last saw each other. Ted's and my wedding, to be exact. Serenah and John had come down from Albany to visit, and John made a fool of himself before they left. He had drunk a few too many glasses of champagne and found himself in an odd predicament when he almost hit her right in front of Ted. My husband, the gentleman he was, caught his fist mid-air and stopped John mid-swing. They left that same night to a hotel until they flew out early the next day.

As we released from our hug, Serenah smiled at me. Her eyes glossed over and she looked as if she was about to cry at any moment. "I'm so happy you made it."

"Me too! It feels great getting out of Tampa, even if it is cold and snowy." That was the truth. Whether it was the near-death experience I just had on the plane or sheer relief from getting out of that same town I had been stuck in for years, I felt amazing. Wrapping her arm around my shoulder, she said,

"Come inside and let me get you some coffee. Hey, did you try The Coffee Bean and Tea Leaf place in Seattle?"

Reaching behind me, I found the handle of my suitcase and yanked it up into the doorway. We went inside. "I did. They had this peppermint latte that was delicious."

Serenah's face distorted as if she could taste the drink herself. "Really? That sounds kind of gross."

"If you like candy canes, it's yummy."

As we got inside the foyer, Charlie walked in from the kitchen and slid his hand to the small of Serenah's back. Reaching his other one out, he introduced himself. "I'm Charlie."

Smiling, I replied, "Nice to finally meet you, Charlie. I'm Angie. I would've recognized you anywhere, though, with all the photos Serenah posts online of you guys."

"Oh, you saw wedding ones we uploaded?" Serenah
asked.

I nodded in agreement. "They were all beautifully
done."

Maneuvering around me and over to my suitcase,
Charlie grabbed it. "Let me take this stuff to your
room."

"Thank you." He smiled and took the suitcase down
a set of stairs off the foyer.

Walking with Serenah, we came around the fireplace
and into the living room. My eyes traced the lines of
the corners up to the vaulted ceiling and over to the
windows. Below the windows were French doors and
a view of the lake. Frozen, but still marvelous, the
lake captured my attention immediately. "It's so
gorgeous here, Serenah."

"I know." We walked across the carpet that led over to the French doors. Peering through the panes of glass and out to the water, she continued, "I've been here for a while now and it never gets old. I love it." A cough came from somewhere behind us. Turning around, I saw the end of a blanket slip past a corner wall and into the kitchen. "Who's that?" I asked with a lowered voice.

Serenah came closer and lowered her voice to a whisper, matching mine. "That's Emma, Charlie's grandma. She lives with us now. She moved in about a month ago since she's toward the end of her life." Frowning, I said, "That must be hard."

"It really is." Serenah let out a sigh as she appeared to be somewhere else in her mind for a moment. Tears began to well in her eyes. "I've grown to love her like Ne Ma."

"Wow," I replied with a raised eyebrow. Ne Ma was our great-grandmother whom all of us cousins would stay with around holidays and during the summer. It was the best place in the world to a kid, not just because of the river running through the property that we always played in, but the warmth and love we shared for Ne Ma. She was a woman who would spend hours playing hide and seek in the woods with us and let us help can strawberry jam in her basement, and she would always keep us loaded up on the sugary sweets during our stay.

"The doctors are saying maybe a couple more months." Serenah looked over her shoulder. "She thinks a little longer, but we'll see. Regardless, she's here now."

Nodding, I said, "Ted's mother just passed a few months back."

Serenah frowned at hearing the words. "So many people are dying lately. I'm sorry to hear that. How did you do at the funeral?"

Shrugging a shoulder as I felt a knot of anxiety ball up in my chest, I kept my eyes on the lake.

"You didn't go." Serenah stepped closer as my eyes watered. Placing an arm around me, she leaned her head against my shoulder. "It's okay, Angie. Sometimes we can't do things."

Though I wasn't sure why, maybe because I felt comfortable with her, the flood gates of my tear ducts broke open and I cried into her shoulder. "It was his mom! I should have been there."

Serenah wrapped her arm around my shoulder. "This is why you should be here. We need this kind of thing. I know I do. Hey, why don't we have some hot cocoa?"

Wiping my eyes, I sniffled and nodded to her. Walking through the dining room, I caught a glimpse of snow falling outside as the light of the day was dwindling. *Wonder if that's the storm we were in?* I thought to myself as we went up a singular step and into the kitchen.

Watching Serenah as she went over to the cupboard, I saw her pull down coffee mugs. One was a candy cane mug, and I felt my pocket where I had placed the candy cane the stranger had given me. I thought about telling her what happened. Sitting down on a stool at the island in the kitchen, I was about to speak when Charlie came in.

"We're going to get dumped on pretty good tonight," Charlie said as he walked through the kitchen and over to Serenah.

"Oh, yeah? How much?" Serenah said as she poured

milk into the mugs. He came over and planted a kiss on her cheek, causing her to light up with a smile. Pulling up his sleeves on his sweater, he crossed his arms and leaned against the doorway that led down a back hallway.

"Couple of feet," he replied. "I told Dylan if it's a good amount, I'll help him build a fort for the boogers in a couple of days."

"Boogers?" I asked.

Serenah laughed and threw a fake swat Charlie's way. He dodged it with a smile. "Children. He *means* children."

"That'll be fun for them." The warm smell of chocolate rose into my nose, warming the cold that still lingered from my trek down the driveway. Charlie came over to the island in the middle of the kitchen and leaned his arm against it as he talked to

Serenah and me. "My dad, when we were kids, would build us igloos and slides out of the snow all the time."

"Really?" Serenah asked. "My dad worked all the time."

Charlie nodded. "Mine too, but he'd get home from work and change before going outside. He'd work outside on the slide until late into the night."

"Wow . . . seems like a dedicated dad." Serenah took a drink of her cocoa.

Shrugging a shoulder, Charlie smiled. "I think he enjoyed the slides and igloos just as much as we did." Laughing, he went over to the cupboard and pulled down a cup. Taking it over to the coffee pot in the kitchen, he poured himself a cup.

As the warmth worked down my throat and filled me with heat, I began feeling the drowsy effects of riding on planes all day. Letting out a yawn, I glanced over at Serenah. "I've got to get some sleep. I'm jet lagged."

"Really? Charlie was going to build a fire here in a few."

Charlie shook his head. "That's fine. Let the girl sleep. She's been through a rough day in the air, I'm sure."

Serenah led me to my room downstairs after a tour of the inn. Walking into the room that would be mine over the course of the next five weeks, I was overwhelmed by the size and amenities that filled it—bath salts near the Jacuzzi, candles strategically placed around the room, a large bed, and a breathtaking view of the ice-covered lake. I was floored with the extravagance. "This is amazing, Serenah," I said as I walked over to the bathroom

door and peeked in, flipping the light switch on. A
standing shower and high ceilings made the
bathroom feel spacious.

"Hope you enjoy it. There's Netflix on the TV if you
get bored." Serenah went to leave the room, but I
stopped her.

"Serenah?"

"Yeah?" she replied, turning at the doorway.

Walking over to her, I looked into her eyes. "Thank
you for having me come here. Since I'm going to be
staying until after Christmas, is there any chance
there's some kind of part-time work or volunteer
stuff I could do around here or with Charlie and his
construction business? I don't want to be cooped up
all day like I was in Tampa."

"We're glad you came. Don't you have a business in
Tampa to run remotely?"

Shrugging, I shook my head. "Not really. Robert is the V.P. and runs the operations entirely. I don't do anything. That's how Ted had it arranged in his company succession plan. Anyway, a daily distraction would help."

Slowly nodding, Serenah looked up at the ceiling as she appeared to contemplate. "I would suggest helping out at the inn, but that would still be cooped up."

"You know me too well."

"Yes I do. I'm sure Charlie can find something. I'll talk to him about it. Okay?"

"Thank you. If you do need any help day to day around here, just let me know. I'm not opposed to helping out."

Going over to my suitcase against the wall, I pulled it onto my bed and opened it. *I'm so tired,* I thought to myself, pulling out my pajamas.

CHAPTER 3

Rolling over in bed the next morning, I looked out to the lake. The image of the snow falling just outside the frosted window with the lake in the backdrop filled me with awestruck wonder of God's beautiful design. Out of the corner of my eye, I saw my suitcase leaning against the wall near the window. That gift the stranger had given me that I had yet to open was calling out to me. *How did I forget about that?*

Slipping from underneath the covers, I scurried over to the suitcase. I grabbed it and tossed it on top of the rumpled comforter and sheets. Unzipping the suitcase, I opened it up and grabbed the box from underneath my favorite pair of jeans. I slipped a finger under the flap until it met a piece of tape, which I ripped off.

Opening the box, I pulled out the card and looked at it.

Gordon Housewares.

No name for the stranger. I set the card to the side and looked into the box and saw the gift as it hid in the shadow of the cardboard construct. As I slid it out, I tilted my head and marveled. It was a clear glass ornament with two children ice skating on a frozen lake. One child was in a blue pair of snow gear, the other in pink. Smiling, I lifted it up and turned it in my hand as I inspected the craftsmanship.

Suddenly, a knock came from my room's door and

Serenah opened the door an inch.

"Can I come in?" she asked. Her eyes widened as it caught the oversized ornament in my hand. "What's that?" she asked, walking in and over to the bed.

"An ornament."

"Well, duh," she said with a laugh. "Where'd it come from?"

I told her all that had happened on the plane—the man, the near-death experience, and the prayer. "And he gave me this as a gift."

She reached her hand out for me to give it over to her to inspect. "Wow . . . this is awesome. We'll have to hang it up when we decorate the tree after Thanksgiving."

"No," I replied, my heart clinging to my ribcage at the notion. "I don't think that'd be good. I know he died a while ago . . ."

Serenah remained quiet.

I took it as a sign of disapproval. "Ted wouldn't like it." Taking the ornament back from her hands, I looked at it. "It just doesn't feel right."

She stood up and raised her hands. "I didn't say anything."

"You didn't have to." Carefully placing the ornament back into the box, I closed the lid and set it on the nightstand beside my bed. I stood and went over to the window.

"Just because we hang the ornament from another man, it doesn't mean we're forgetting Ted ever existed." Serenah's words were gentle, caring. Watching the snow fall, I said, "I know I've hung on longer than I should . . ."

Walking up to my side, she put her hand on my shoulder. "You should get out there and meet new people. Mingle around a bit. You mentioned the man gave you his card and number. It wouldn't be the worst thing to text him."

I looked at her as my eyes glistened with a layer of tears. *Why, after all these years, do I still feel like he would be disappointed?* I wondered. "I still think about Ted, Serenah."

"Maybe it'll help if you *try* to hang out with new guys." I knew her intentions were pure. She was just trying to help, and the idea of getting out there in the dating world both terrified and excited me. Shrugging, I replied, "Maybe you're right."

"I'm not trying to downplay your situation if you're still grieving."

Shaking my head, I said, "I know. I'm not still grieving. There's just a strange void in my life now. I want to date. I want to get out there . . . I just don't know how. It's been so long. I'm sure I would be very awkward going out nowadays."

"You know who you might want to have a chat with sometime?" she asked, her voice gentle.

Looking over at her, I raised my eyebrows. "Who?"

"Emma. She lost her husband quite a while ago. I'm sure she has a bit of wisdom she's gleaned from the experience. She's helped me a few times."

Nodding, I looked back at the lake. "I'll keep that in mind." My eyes couldn't help but keep looking outside as snow and ice weren't something I was accustomed to back in Tampa. They had a peaceful way about them, and even though I didn't care for the blistering cold experience I had coming out of the airport, I enjoyed them from the inside looking out. "I knew you had snow up here, and I've seen pictures you've put on Facebook, but I had no idea how beautiful it truly is in person."

"I guess that's why people dream of a white Christmas, as the song goes."

Serenah left to go make us breakfast, and I stayed a little longer in my room. I fetched my Bible from my suitcase and sat in the nook below the window to read my daily Scriptures, and then I prayed. *Thank you, Lord, for Your Word today. Thank You, Lord, for having me come up here. Help me to understand Your will for my life. Thank You for keeping me safe during the flight. Even though my faith faltered, You did not. Thank You for placing amazing people in my life like Serenah. I pray that you keep my paths aligned with Yours. In Your heavenly name, I pray, Amen.*

That evening, guests arrived at the inn for a dinner

that Serenah had told me about earlier that day.

They were not guests to the inn per se, but instead

friends of Charlie and Serenah. They all had agreed

to meet to celebrate the Thanksgiving holiday a

couple of days prior to the actual day since so many

had family obligations on the day of. A traditional

turkey, mashed potatoes and gravy, and my personal

favorite—stuffing— were all in the works

throughout the day leading up to dinner.

Snow had lightly begun to fall outside just before the

five o'clock hour when everyone was due to show

up. My nerves were rattled in anticipation of

meeting everyone Serenah had grown to love over

her time here. I took a hot shower and dabbed

frankincense oil on my wrists and neck. I was

relaxed as much as possible by the time people

began showing up.

"This is my cousin, Angie," Serenah said, introducing me to a woman with blonde hair and a man with brown hair.

Extending a hand and a smile, I greeted them both. The warmth that radiated from the couple was pure, and I instantly felt at ease with the two of them.

"I'm Katie, and this is my boyfriend, Joe."

"Katie and Joe," I repeated back to them to help me remember their names. Repeating names was a trick I picked up along my travels in my early twenties while studying business in college.

I walked beside Katie as we all followed Serenah into the dining room. Serenah split off back to the kitchen while Joe went over to Charlie to help organize the tables to form one big table in the center of the dining room.

"You're from Florida, right?" Katie's eyes were on the guys as they worked.

"Yeah. I wanted to get out of the house for the holidays."

"Don't be bashful. Be *real*. Your apartment caught fire," Serenah hollered with a laugh from the kitchen. Katie covered her mouth and her eyes widened. Her and Serenah's eyes met. "Where's your brother, Katie? We can't eat until everyone is here."

"He couldn't make it—some business meeting or something." Katie turned back to me. "I moved out to Newport to live a couple of months ago. Serenah convinced me it was only smart to get away from the hustle and bustle of the city."

Smiling, I asked, "Do you like it out here?"

Katie nodded. "I love the people. It's where I grew up. Outside of that, though, it's a peaceful area and doesn't have a lot of crime like in Spokane. I do miss the Spokane Falls just outside my window, but I have a lake a few minutes away now."

"And you have me pretty close," Joe added with a grin in our direction.

Katie smiled. "Very true."

Charlie and Joe finished with the tables and headed into the kitchen. We could faintly hear them over the Christmas music playing. They were inquiring about a tablecloth of some sort from Serenah.

Knocks echoed from the front door moments later, pulling Serenah from the kitchen once again.

More friends arrived.

Soon, the table was set, the food was out, and eating had commenced after a prayer led by Charlie.

Conversations flew back and forth across the table between the friends they had invited, with me contributing little. I didn't know these people, and I wasn't exactly a social butterfly for group settings anyway. It wasn't long after the meal started that someone took notice and pulled me in.

"Serenah tells me you're in the market for a date," Charlotte said as she grabbed a roll from a basket beside the turkey.

Flush with embarrassment, my cheeks went bright red. "Oh yeah? Did you hear that?"

Katie put her arm on my shoulder. "You should get out there. It can be fun getting to know different people."

Finishing her bite, Charlotte wiped her mouth with a napkin as she nodded. "My husband didn't *die,* but he did leave me. I got lucky and met Dylan when he moved next door, but I should have been putting myself out there. Not dating, really, but just getting to know people."

Taking a sip of my lemon water, I set the glass down. "I'm only here for five weeks. It wouldn't be fair to get into a relationship."

Serenah spoke up. "Since you're not in Tampa, you could go on dates and have zero long-term commitment."

"But really, what's the point of that?" I asked. "As Christians, we're supposed to date in anticipation of marriage."

"True," Miley said. "But you can at least get out there and see what the dating world is like nowadays. If you find a guy you really like, you could figure out a long-distance relationship. But honestly, this will just be a trial run to get you used to meeting new people again. Believe me . . . I'm still single, and it's difficult to converse with strangers."

Charlotte stood up and came around the table to me. Bending down on her knees, she showed me a picture. "This guy is a buddy of Dylan's. Really cute, quiet, and he likes to read."

Nodding, I forced a smile. "I see."

Katie pulled her phone out and showed me a picture. "This is the youth pastor at Pines Baptist. I don't know much about him."

Taking a deep breath, I let out a sigh.

Serenah grabbed everyone's attention. "Hey now, leave her be. Just send her their names on Facebook and she'll look them up or something if she wants to."

Glancing over at her, I smiled and mouthed the words, 'Thank you,' almost forgiving her for even telling her friends I needed to date in the first place. Sometimes, Serenah was *too* helpful.

As dinner wound down and everyone left, I was feeling a bit over-stimulated by all the conversations around the dinner table—especially the one about me dating. Going out on a date sounded humorous. I hadn't dated in years, and the idea of getting to know someone all over again sounded exhausting, yet I know I didn't want to spend the rest of my life alone. *Could I really go on dates?* I wondered as I sat on the couch drinking a cup of coffee as Serenah and Charlie recounted the dinner and how everything turned out delicious.

"I found something for you to do to keep busy if you're still interested," Charlie said, breaking into my thoughts.

Raising an eyebrow as an indicator to continue, I looked over at him.

"The Christmas tree lot. You could start the day after

Thanksgiving. It's at the grocery store, right up the road in Newport."

"I'll do it," I replied, beaming with a smile as I thought about helping families pick out trees for their homes.

CHAPTER 4

Arriving at the Newport grocery store's tree lot the day after Thanksgiving, an older gentleman, probably in his late sixties or early seventies, was fastening a plank of wood to the wire fence just outside the lot. As his arm moved, I could see the word, *OPEN*, painted crookedly but clearly on the wood. A few Boy Scouts could be seen through an opening in the fence in the distance. They would be helping out too. It was all volunteer work, according to what Charlie had explained over eggs and hash browns earlier that morning. All the proceeds, after the costs of operation, went to the Toys for Tots foundation that operated in Spokane and the surrounding area, a local charity that helped the poor and needy during the holidays.

Pulling into a parking stall near the gate's entrance, Serenah put the car into park and pointed out the old man. "That's Mr. Atkins. He's part of the founding families of Newport and will be your boss." As he turned to acknowledge our vehicle, he broke into a wide grin at the sight of Serenah. She seemed to have a lot of pull around here with the locals even though she hadn't lived in the area very long. It was easy to tell she had grown on anyone and everyone she came into contact with. That was what she had always been like, though. Even as kids, on the playgrounds at the parks, she'd be the first to make friends with everyone around.

Fidgeting with the corner of my coat as my anxiety

rose inside my chest, I wondered if I really had what it took to work again after years of not lifting little more than a few fingers on a keyboard to reply to a simple email from the VP.

"You okay?" Serenah asked, looking over at me.

Glancing over, I flashed her a curt nod. "Just nervous."

"You'll do *fine*. They appreciate any help they can get. In their mind, you're a blessing."

Peering back at the Boy Scouts who couldn't be a day over thirteen, I knew I would be. "I know."

Pulling on the door handle, I got out. Serenah provided me with all the clothing I could imagine to help keep me warm at the tree lot—a couple of layers of shirts underneath a coat, gloves, jeans, and a pair of snow pants. It wasn't snowing that morning, but there was a bite in the air from the coolness that gnawed at my exposed face, reminding me of my Florida roots. Slush moved loosely beneath my boots as I made my way over to the gentleman at the gate.

Glancing back at Serenah, I waved as she pulled out of the parking stall.

"You must be Angie." The man's voice reminded me of a rugged cowboy from an old western movie. Turning around, I shook hands with him. "You're Mr. Atkins, right?"

"You can call me Don." He motioned with a wave for me to follow as he walked through the opening into the tree lot. "This isn't rocket science here. People look at trees, give you some money, and you help them get it to their car." He lifted a worn leathery glove that protected his hand and pointed toward the corner of the tree lot. "Back there is where Kim and Travis drop off new trees."

He stopped and turned around. Glancing at me from head to toe, he tapped his chin for a moment, almost shooting me a glare. "You strong enough to do this? Carry trees and whatnot?"

Shrugging a shoulder, I said, "I own a soap factory back in Tampa. I've moved quite a few boxes and equipment back in the glory days of start up."

He turned his head and spit and then nodded as his eyes rounded back to me. "In that case, you should be okay. Don't hurt yourself trying to lift something. If it's too heavy, ask someone for help."

"Okay."

He raised a hand. "That's not sexist. I tell everyone that. Trying to cover my bases. I don't need no lawsuit right now with all the finances being poured into—" He paused. "Well, never mind." Walking over to a small fold-out table, he pointed to a silver box with a lock. "That's the cash box. I have the key, and if I'm not here, Chip will have it. He hangs out in the warm trailer right up yonder." He jerked his head and pointed over to the trailer. Then his eyes moved past me and a smile came across his face. "Our first customers have arrived. You can shadow my star pupil, Micah, until you learn the ropes." Letting out a holler, he called for the boy. "Micah!"

A boy about the age of twelve came over to us. His face kept a serious look about it, and his Boy Scout hat sat squarely on his head.

"I'm Angie. Nice to meet you."

"Micah." He shook my hand and smiled, but it fell from his face almost immediately as he saw Don's face not smiling. He looked to be attempting to imitate the older gentleman. Following the boy, we went over to the customer.

The idea of working at the tree lot seemed like it would be fun, but once I got three hours in, I realized it wasn't the greatest. Between sap covering my hands, having to take my gloves off for a better grip, and the runny nose that would never cease due to being outside, I was ready to go home when Don finally let me leave around noon. The best part of it was the little sips of conversation I'd find myself in with Micah through the shift when Don wasn't around. If it weren't for the kid and for a good cause, I would have probably quit.

Late that afternoon, before the sun began to set back at the inn, Serenah and I went for a walk. Though I'd had a miserable time out in the brutal elements at

the tree lot earlier in the day, it couldn't keep me

from wanting to get outside and enjoy the

afternoon. The air was still chilly outside, even with

all the layers of clothing she had lent me, but at least

I wasn't going to be hauling any trees around in it.

Following behind Serenah as we made our way

down the slippery ice rink of stairs that Charlie

hadn't de-iced yet, I clutched onto the railing for

dear life. Every step felt loose and unsecured

beneath my feet, but I kept going. Toward the

bottom, I had become a little more relaxed with my

grip on the railing, and a foot slid out from

underneath me entirely. I let out a scream and

tightly wrapped my arms around the railing as the

other foot left the step. My back was inches from the

stairs and my heart was beating so furiously, I

thought I was on the verge of a heart attack. Serenah turned around and let out a laugh, covering her mouth.

"You okay?" she asked, pulling down her pink scarf from her lips as her laughter slowed to a dull roar.

"Yeah, right! Why are these so stinking slick?" I asked as I recomposed myself and got my footing.

"Charlie should de-ice those."

"I'll remind him. With fewer guests around the holidays, he forgets these back stairs," Serenah said with a little laughter still in her tone. We continued down to the snow covered yard below with no more near-death experiences. The snow down in the yard was at least a foot deep thanks to the snow drift off the roof of the inn. My legs began to feel the burn as the muscles screamed out at me, begging for me to rest.

Soon enough, we were out of the yard and into the woods that separated the inn from the neighbor on the side. As we entered the woods, the deep snow thankfully tapered. Instead of the forest floor, the snow stuck to tree branches overhead and caused the branches to bow. Hearing a branch snap in the distance a minute into the walk, I peered up and saw snow flurrying down through the pine trees. The overall quiet outdoors brought a relaxation over my entire body.

Serenah looked over her shoulder. "Just a little bit further."

I didn't know where we were going, but I was having a great time outside of the step incident. Our journey only lasted a minute or two longer, and then we arrived at a small tree that wasn't more than four feet in height. Serenah walked right up to it and put a knee down. Her pink glove glided against the little branches of the tree, and a dusting of snow flaked off, tumbling delicately to the ground. Serenah peered over at me with glistening eyes. "This is my baby's tree."

Like a snowball hitting me in the side of the head, I recalled the child she had lost when she first moved out west. Coming over to her side, I got down on my knees and hugged her with an arm.

She looked at me and said, "You already know John went to prison, but I didn't tell you what happened shortly thereafter."

"What happened?"

"He was stabbed and killed."

My eyes widened. "Really?"

She nodded as her eyes went back to the tree.

"Apparently, they don't like woman beaters in

prison. Some guy stabbed him twelve times."

"I was a little worried he was going to get out and come after you again."

She laughed a little and nodded as she pulled off her glove to wipe her eyes of the tears. "I heard that *a lot* when he went away."

Our eyes both went back to the tree for a moment longer as a comfortable silence came between us. Serenah looked over at me. "I'm sorry if last night made you uncomfortable with everybody trying to give you dating advice. I wasn't thinking when I mentioned it."

Shaking my head, I let out a breath of air. "Honestly, I think it helped me. I need to get out of my shell."

My eyes fell to the tree again as Serenah put her glove on. "We should pray."

"Okay." Serenah reached over to hold my hand.

As snow lightly began to fall between the trees above our heads, we bowed our heads and our hearts.

Serenah led the prayer.

"We come to You today, Father, seeking Your face. Seeking Your love. You are the Great Comforter, the One and only that can bring us joy during hardship. Please help us be still and know You are God. Though we don't understand the bad that sometimes happens in this life, help us to lean on You in those times. We also pray for Emma as she's preparing to come meet You. We pray these things in Your name, Amen."

Standing up after the prayer, Serenah shook her head as her eyes began to water and she turned to me. "I love you, Angie. I'm sorry I wasn't there for you when Ted passed."

"Oh, Serenah," I replied, shaking my head as tears fell down my cheeks. "No, I'm sorry I haven't been here for *you*." My eyes gravitated toward where we had come from and then back at her. "You moved on from John, and I'm so proud of you for doing that. It's amazing. I loved your mother dearly, but her advice about staying with that evil man was—"

"I know. She was wrong." Serenah nodded. "You're going to be okay, Angie. You know that? You'll find someone who loves you the way you need to be loved."

"Maybe." Ted was gone, but I was ready to meet someone new. I knew that. My thoughts drifted to the picture of that youth pastor that Katie showed me. I thought about how he had a cute smile. *Maybe I'll message him?*

That night, I retired to my room early and pulled out my laptop. Sitting crisscross on the bed, I logged into Facebook. Messages were sitting in my inbox from both Katie and Charlotte with links to those guys' profiles. Adjusting on my bed, I clicked into Katie's guy first. Clicking through, I learned of his name—Peter. Scrolling down, I saw he enjoyed teaching youth group and helping the homeless. *Seems too good to be true. Only one way to find out!* Clicking *Add*, I closed the laptop and prayed for God's guidance as even friending him felt awkward. One was enough for tonight.

As I lifted my eyes from prayer, I saw the ornament box sitting on my nightstand. I had forgotten about that stranger on the plane and the business card he left in the box. Leaning over the bed, I pulled the box to me and searched for his card. Not finding it, I checked the sheets and covers. Still no card. Going to the floor, I searched on all fours. *Where is it?* Then I checked under the bed.

There, in plain sight, it lay.

Reaching, I grabbed it and sat back onto my knees.

It had a cellphone number on it so I texted him.

Me: Hi . . . this is airplane girl, Lol. Want to meet up?

After I hit *Send*, I stared at my cellphone screen for a solid five minutes until my feet went numb because of the way I was sitting. I sat on the edge of the bed and began biting on a nail. *Will he ever text back?* I wondered.

CHAPTER 5

He never texted back that night. As I sipped on my morning coffee the next day and caught a glimpse of the morning news, my thoughts drifted back to that plane ride we had shared. We were dropping through clouds in a silver bullet, heading for certain death. Perhaps the prayer and his being there in that moment were just like the gift he had given me—a gift.

A story came on the news that morning that strung Serenah and I along with smiles as we watched—a rare treat for any newscast. It was a story of a local woman in Spokane who had just lost her husband in

Iraq. With little money and far less hope, she hadn't

a clue how she would pay for the gifts she had

placed on layaway for her children earlier that year.

Yesterday, when she went down to the store to take

the items off layaway, she had discovered someone

paid for it all. A stranger. My heart warmed, and I

glanced over to see Serenah wiping a stray tear as

she smiled.

The front door opened and closed, followed by a

stomping sound as Charlie kicked the snow from his

boots. Walking around the fireplace, he came into

the living room. "I got the tree." He surveyed the

room. "You ready for it?"

"Yes, dear," Serenah replied as she looked over to

him.

Charlie left back outside to go grab the tree, and my

phone buzzed with a notification. Setting my cup

down on the coaster at the end of the couch, I picked it up.

Stranger: How about today? Meet at the North Town Mall at four.

Wow. He texted me back, I thought. *And he has a plan for us.* My face couldn't help but break into a wide grin as I read the text.

"What?" Serenah asked.

I flashed her the text and her eyes widened. Slapping my leg playfully, she said, "Look at you go, Angie!"

Laughing, I shook my head. "Whatever . . . it's just friends."

Me: That'll work. Just as friends though.

Stranger: Ha-ha. As you wish.

Charlie made his way back inside, huffing and grunting as he pulled the massive tree through the foyer and into the living room. A trail of pine needles followed closely behind him. Serenah's eyes caught the mess he was making.

"You'd better clean those up," Serenah warned playfully.

"Sure." He glanced toward the back of the tree and shook his head as sweat beaded on his forehead. Looking back to Serenah, he said, "Come help me, please." Charlie held a huff to his tone as he was most likely exhausted by the time he got the tree into the living room.

"Don't you dare try to take a tone with me, Mister," Serenah retorted, laughing as she set her cup down on a coaster. "Just *had* to have the ten-foot tree, didn't you?" He smiled as his eyes narrowed on her.

My eyes surveyed the massive tree as he held it,

waiting for Serenah to make it over to him.

Serenah laughed, trying to cut through the dry

sarcasm. Making it over to Charlie, she rubbed his

back. "Mr. Atkins said Jody *always* got this big of a

tree. If Wayne could haul it inside every year, you

can too. You work construction, Charlie."

He smiled. "Okay. Okay. You got me there." His eyes

ran along the tree as it lay on its side. "All we have

to do is get it upright."

Jumping up, I set my cup down and came over. "I

can help."

All three of us worked together to get the tree up

and placed in front of the fireplace. Standing back,

Serenah beamed as Charlie grimaced.

"Guess no chestnuts are going to be roasting over an

open fire this year," Charlie said.

Serenah playfully smacked him. "Oh, stop. We'll

move it over here." She pointed over to the wall that

ran between the kitchen and dining room. "We just

need to move that table out."

Hurrying over, I grabbed the table and placed it out

of the way near the dining room. We all three

moved the tree over. Standing back, we all nodded

in approval of the final result.

"I love it." Serenah's eyes scanned over it and the

room as she backed up more.

"Me too," Charlie added.

"Me three." Smiling over at them, I knew it would be

a great Christmas.

"Angie, come help me grab the Christmas lights and

ornaments." Following behind Serenah, we went in

through the kitchen and down the hallway to her

private quarters. Cutting through her living room, she went over to a closet door and opened it. Going inside the closet, she turned around. Taking a deep breath, she grabbed my hands and held them as she looked me in the eyes. "Please let us hang that gorgeous ornament."

Letting out a laugh, I shook my head. "I don't know, Serenah . . ."

"He's just a guy. Who cares?" Grabbing the box of Christmas lights from the top shelf, she turned and handed it to me.

I took the box and nodded. "True. We'll hang it."

Serenah clapped excitedly. "You're the best."

Turning around, I headed out to the living room with a smile on my face. As I walked with the box of lights, I thought about seeing him later that day. *What if it's weird? I haven't dated in years. Wait. It's*

not a date. It's just as friends. It'll be fine. My surety
of how the time with the stranger would unfold was
unclear, but I took comfort in the fact that he was a
fellow believer.

Fully dressed and ready to go by two, I had an hour
before I could leave so I took the opportunity to
spend additional time seeking the Lord. Taking my
Bible, I headed upstairs and read on the couch since
Serenah was in town at the grocery store. The quiet
of the inn was sublime compared to the everlasting
distractions that sounded outside my apartment
back in Tampa. By the time Serenah made it back to
the inn, my anxieties and cares had all been cast on
the Lord and I was ready, mostly, to go see the

stranger.

I retrieved my purse from the side of the couch as Serenah came in with grocery bags in each hand. She looked at me with a smile. "You look hot."

Wearing a white pea coat, black leggings and a fun, festive red shirt, I had dressed for a date even though I was trying not to think of it as one.

I laughed. "Am I too dressed up?"

She passed into the kitchen, and I could hear a snicker echo through the doorway. "It's fine."

"All right." Retrieving my frankincense oil from my purse, I dabbed a couple of dots on my wrists and then my neck. The aroma permeated the area around me. My eyes fell on the tree and the ornament he had given me.

Placing the oil back in my purse, I checked the time and saw it was time to leave. As I stood up, Serenah came out of the kitchen and handed me her car

keys. Then, putting her hands on my shoulders, she

looked into my eyes. "Remember, just relax and have

some fun. It's not a date."

Exhaling a large breath through my nose, I said,

"Thank you."

Snow had started to fall lightly on the way into

town, but the roads were all clear. As I turned off the

GPS on my phone at the sight of the North Town

Mall only a block away on Division Street, I took a

few deep breaths to clear my mind. *It's not a date.*

Pulling into the parking lot, my heart pounded as I

saw multiple entryways into the parking garage.

Parking at the curb along one of the entrances, I

texted him asking where he had parked.

Stranger: J7

Seeing the entrance right in front of me, I continued driving and turned in. As I climbed up the ramps in the garage, I surveyed the rows of cars for him.

There he was.

In a pair of jeans and a button up long-sleeved shirt, he looked casual but classy.

I waved. *Why'd I just wave?* I wondered, feeling my cheeks go flush as I pulled into the empty stall beside him. While I was getting out of my car, he came around the end to greet me. He pulled out a small bouquet of yellow roses from behind his back, bowed slightly, and handed them to me. "For you, Miss." Flicking his eyebrows up, he said, "Yellow roses symbolize *Friendship*, or so I hear."

"Thank you." Smelling a whiff of roses, I smiled.

"They're lovely." Turning back to my car, I set them on the driver seat. As I shut the door and locked my car, footsteps and light conversation between a mother and child could be heard. Glancing around, we spotted a family of five walking by. A little boy with blond hair waved at me as our eyes connected. Smiling at him, I waved back.

"You like kids?" the stranger asked as the family continued down the ramp of the parking garage.

"How about names first?" I laughed. "I'm Angie."

"Angie, short for Angela?"

"Yes, but no one calls me Angela."

"Angela, nice to formally meet you. I'm Connor."

"Nice to finally know your name. And of course I like kids. Do you?" We began walking. We were only a few paces behind the family. Usually, I minded when someone called me Angela, but I couldn't bring myself to care with Connor. I actually liked how it sounded when he said it.

"Yeah. Whenever I need a reminder of how life really should work, I stop in by the toddler's class at church and hang out with the littles. Outside of eating their own boogers and the occasional poop in the pants, they get this thing called life better than most adults. It brings me back into focus and reminds me what really matters in life."

Laughing, I ran my fingers through my hair and pulled the hair caught under my pea coat out. "So you're a philosopher?"

He smiled and shrugged.

The little boy in front of us turned as he held onto his mom and waved again. Connor waved back and smiled.

Arriving to the door of the mall, Connor picked up his pace and held the door open for the family in front of us and then for me. Our eyes connected as I passed by him holding the door. We both smiled, and a warm sense of security wrapped itself around me. Being near Connor calmed me and made me happy all at once.

Christmas music played throughout the mall as we strode down the walkway past stores, kiosks and even Santa's North Pole, a place where kids could sit on Santa's lap for a picture. Connor was taking me somewhere in the mall, but he hadn't yet revealed where we were going. As we walked, we pointed out stores we liked and even stopped at a booth with freshly made fudge and got a sample.

As we came around the corner towards the food

court, smells of cinnamon shared the air with the Christmas melodies. The smell brought a smile to my heart as I recalled the bundle of cinnamon-scented pine cones my mother would buy every year right after Thanksgiving.

Turning another corner, we came up to a green colored carpet that held a musical ensemble. Five musicians, all with instruments and red Santa hats, sat waiting in chairs. Spotting a violinist, I smiled.

Connor pushed up his coat sleeve for the time. "Any moment now."

The violinist stood up and centered herself in front of the group. Her hair was long and pulled back in a tight ponytail. She looked poised and in complete control of her body. She held the violin up against her neck.

The other musicians behind the violinist began

playing 'O Holy Night'. Joy filled me at the familiar

sounds as they hummed against not only my

eardrums, but my heart.

Then the violin started in.

Leaning into Connor's ear, I said quietly, "I love

this."

He turned his head and leaned in close enough to

my ear that I could feel the warmth of his breath.

His scent was sharp and welcoming as I leaned in to

hear better. "I'm glad. I remembered your comment

on the plane."

"You did this?" I asked, surprised.

"Well, kind of. They were already playing. I just

requested them to do a special violin number," he

replied with a smirk.

Wow. What a sweet thing to do, I thought to myself

as I smiled up at him. Listening to the musical

ensemble, I stood beside Connor as passersby gathered around the musicians.

CHAPTER 6

Connor took me a few blocks down to a nice restaurant after the mall. He held the door open for me as we went inside and waited for me to sit down first before he sat. He was a gentleman. I liked that. After our meal, we began chatting about our lives. Instantly, we found common ground. We were both entrepreneurs. Connor owned a plastic ware company, and Ted and I—well, just me now— owned an organic soap factory.

"This whole movement of minimum wage driving you nuts as much as it is me?" Connor asked and then took a sip of his water. His voice was warm against my ear drums. His words carried weight and conviction.

"It drives me mad!" I threw my head back and laughed, recalling the email I received a few months back. There was a petition that went around the factory that a dozen or so employees signed. They were demanding a raise or they'd quit. I told Connor about it.

"What'd you end up doing?" he asked, leaning across the table as his eyes begged for me to continue. The attention was nice. He was nice. Everything about him was making me warm up to the idea of being with someone again. Something closer than friends. A devilish smile crept into the corner of my lips. "I called their bluff. I told them I'd move the entire company overseas and pay children pennies to do their jobs if they didn't want them. That was the end."

Connor's mouth gaped open for a moment before he covered it with a hand and leaned into his palm as his elbow was pivoted on the table. A smile hid behind his hand. He liked that, I could tell. Dropping his hand away from his mouth a moment or two later, he shook his head. "You've got some . . . backbone."

I laughed, knowing what he meant. His phone rang, pulling his attention away from our conversation. He checked the screen and then slid out of the booth. "It'll just be a moment."

He wandered to the hallway a few feet away and spoke for a few minutes before returning to our table. "Mr. Important," I said with a smirk. He smiled forcefully and took a drink of his water.

"Work never ends when you own your own business, does it?"

I shook my head. "Not if we don't allow it to end . . ."

After our dinner at The Mustard Seed, we headed down to Riverfront Park. The water wasn't entirely frozen over by the gripping coldness of winter, but there were plenty of spots you could see ice formed on top. The park was relatively quiet. Not a lot of people walked the paths and across the bridges. We passed by a few carolers, and Connor gave them a hundred-dollar bill.

His desire to help warmed a part of me. He was a good man.

We came to a bridge across a part of the river that had the Spokane Falls. The sounds of the roaring ice cold water made a part of me uncomfortable. I reached out and grabbed his arm. I wasn't for certain if he'd pull away, but I was relieved when he didn't. Snuggling in closer to his side at the falls, we looked out at the falls for a few moments without any words. Many people couldn't enjoy the lack of conversation. I knew I could, but now I was finding out that Connor could too.

"You think about that airplane ride a lot?" I asked, my head pressed against his arm.

He took a moment before speaking. "It was terrifying, but yes. I think of it often. It was one of the most impactful moments of my life. I thought we were dead."

That word—dead. I hated it. It reminded me of Ted. Though I had moved on from my late husband and the wounds were mostly done away with, the word was still a trigger for me. I didn't like it. Connor noticed I had become upset and gently backed me up at arm's length to connect with my eyes.

"What's wrong?" he asked.

Shaking my head, I wiped my eyes. A blush blossomed on my cheeks. Feeling embarrassed, I tried to shrug it off, but he insisted I tell him what was wrong so I did. I told him about how I had lost Ted a couple of weeks before Christmas a few years ago. I was brief with him.

"I had no idea." Connor's head hung and his shoulders slumped as he moved over to the railing on the bridge. He rested his hands on the railing and turned to look at me. "I know the comparison is probably zilch, but I just lost my best friend this last summer. We grew up together."

My heart broke for him in that moment as his softer side came out. Closing the gap of pavement between us, I rested a hand on Connor's back as his eyes returned to the falls and he continued. "He had a wife and kids." He stopped there even though there seemed to be more on his mind, on the tip of his tongue.

Rubbing his back in a circular motion, I tried my best to comfort him. I knew it didn't help a whole lot, but it did help when someone seemed to care. "Loss is hard. Perhaps one of the hardest parts of life, Connor. I understand that."

He wiped his eyes and let out a breath of air.

"Want to get warmed up?" Connor asked as we passed by a giant red wagon playground, thankfully changing the subject. I could imagine children playing on the toys when the weather is warm.

"Yes!" I replied.

He tenderly took my hand and led me under a bridge and around a corner to a yellow glowing structure of some sort. My whole body became suddenly aware of how cold it truly was and how warm his hand was. Coming closer to the building, I saw it was an indoor carousel. My jaw began to jitter at how cold I was feeling. Connor wrapped an arm around me as we got closer and rubbed my arm to help bring warmth.

Going inside, he held the door open for me, and the warmth immediately began to thaw the cold that had sunk so deep into my bones. Taking off his beanie cap, Connor's eyes widened as he looked at the colorful painted horses that stood still in the circular room. Softened sounds of childhood rang in the background as a worker down the way opened a gate and let a few teenagers onto the ride.

Snowflakes had melted in my hair, and now water began dripping down the sides of my face. Connor turned to me and gently wiped the water from the side of my face. He motioned with a nod toward the carousel gatekeeper behind him. "Want to go for a ride?"

Taken aback, I laughed and shook my head. "It's for kids."

Connor glanced over at the carousel and then back to me, a boyish grin on his face.

"I don't know . . ." I said.

"Come on, kids can't have all the fun," he insisted, grabbing my hand. The touch of his hand might have been cold, but it sent shockwaves of warmth up my arm. His touch was tender. We hurried around the iron railing and down to the gate. The man was about to latch it when Connor stuck out his hand. "Stop, please. We want on."

After a funny look and a snide remark, the guy let us

through the gate, and soon, we found our way to two majestic steeds that appeared to be frozen in mid-stride.

"I can't believe we're doing this." I laughed as I tightened the belt around my waist.

"Gotta have *a little* fun once in a while. Or what's the point of being an adult and being able to do what you want?" Connor climbed up on his horse with a smile on his face like that of a toddler who just snuck the last cookie from the cookie jar.

Feelings were developing for this man—I could feel it. The way he smiled as the lights over our heads bounced off the mirrors in the middle of the carousel and the way we were looking at each other, we were deepening. First, the smiles to one another and the laughter as we spun in circles, reminding me of a far-off part of my past, somewhere in the

recesses of my mind where childhood resided. Then,
the laughter and smiles stopped while the ride
continued. We looked at each other as the music
continued and our horses rode up and down. Our
souls brushed up against each other in that moment.
I felt it.

The ride stopped, and I thought for certain he was
going to close the gap of space between us right on
the platform of the ride and kiss me, but he didn't.
He put his arm around me and led me off the ride.
As we came off the carousel, I was still in a daze,
almost a little wobbly in my steps. His phone rang
again, but even him taking another phone call for
work couldn't kill the moment entirely. It was too
powerful.

He released his arm from me and walked a few
steps. He turned around to face me and flashed a

smile. He wasn't trying to distance himself, but it seemed to be natural for him.

When the call ended, I pushed him playfully in the shoulder. "You really ought to delegate. Learn to have your people work for you."

"I love working."

Stopping, I turned to him and looked him in the eyes. A spark of that same feeling from the carousel coursed through my veins. I stretched my arms up and rested my hands on his neck as I continued looking at him. "You can love work, but you have to make time for things that are important too."

He smiled and returned a small nod.

Arriving at our parked cars that night in the parking

garage, he asked, "What are you up to Monday?"

"I'm working at a tree lot out in Newport. It's volunteer, but it's for a good cause."

"Really?" Connor had a perplexed look on his face as he took his beanie off and ran his fingers through his hair. "Wait, so *your* cousin you said earlier was Serenah, as in Serenah Dillard? Charlie and Serenah?"

"Yeah." I tilted my head. "Do you know them?"

"Yeah!" Connor smiled. "They're my friends . . . well, kind of. They're more my sister Katie's friends than mine."

"Katie is your sister?" I asked, leaning forward with raised eyebrows. I could hardly believe it. "No way! I sat by her for Thanksgiving dinner."

Connor shot a hand out and nodded. "I was going to be there but got tied up with a business meeting. I can't believe I would have seen you there. I wouldn't have gotten out of it if I'd have known."

Shaking a finger at him as I grinned, I said, "That blasted work keeps you from living life, Connor." I looked him in the eyes.

"I know, I know . . ."

Pulling my keys out from my purse, I smiled at him. He came closer and we hugged. "It was nice hanging out," I said as we released.

"It was lovely," he replied. He began backing up toward his car. "Drive safe tonight."

"You too."

Smiling, I got inside my car and headed back to the inn.

CHAPTER 7

Flipping the sign to *Open* Monday morning, I headed back to the corner of the tree lot to help Kim unload the trees that she had to drop off that day. Travis was out with a cold. No big surprise there. As we unloaded the trees into the lot, Kim looked to have something weighing on her mind. The way she carried herself was different. She was the type of person who beamed with joy and happiness daily. It wasn't that way today.

"You okay, Kim?" I asked as we set a tree down and leaned it against the fence.

Looking at me for a moment as if she debated telling me, she let out a sigh. "Our cat died last night. It's been hard on Amy and Lexi."

"I'm sorry."

She shrugged a shoulder. "It happens." Peering back toward the entrance where we had been hauling the trees, she continued. "I'm hoping this will be the last year with the trees. It's hard getting deliveries out and the pay isn't worth it."

"Why do you guys do it?" I asked.

"The money." She laughed and started walking back to the truck. Stepping up onto the back bumper, Kim reached up and pulled the latch downward, closing it. Hopping off backward, she turned around and looked me in the eyes. "Have a good day, and tell Don 'hello'."

Nodding, I turned and headed back into the tree lot.

Don would be there by eleven. Until then, it was just me. Hearing a car pull up, I took a deep breath and headed down a row of trees to go see who the first customer would be.

To my surprise, it was Connor.

He had a big smile on his face as he stretched out his arms. "I took the day off. *Delegated.*"

"Wow . . ." I grabbed at his pockets. "No phone?"

He shook his head. "No phone at all."

Connor looked good in his long overcoat and suit, but I knew it wouldn't work. Turning my head toward the trailer in the lot, I pointed. "There's a spare pair of overalls and a flannel jacket that belongs to Don. You can use those."

"This won't work?" he asked, glancing over himself.

I shook my head. *He's too cute.* Giving me a nod, he headed into the trailer, and I couldn't help but watch him. Scents of soap and aftershave flooded my senses as he walked by and went into the trailer. He smelled so good. Sounds of a car door startled me out of my daydreaming, and I peeked around the end of the row of trees. A family.

"Hello," I said as they walked inside.

Showing them around, I gave them a set of options and then allowed them time to think it over. Going over to Connor as he came out of the trailer, I couldn't help but let out a laugh.

"Hey," he said, turning red. "This feels weird."

"Looks kind of weird too." I laughed, covering my face. "It's cute too."

He shooed me away with a hand. "Oh, whatever."

He squirmed as he tried to adjust the flannel jacket.

The arms were too short on the jacket, but the

length of the mid-section was fine. It looked sort of

hilarious and I loved it. Once the family picked out a

tree, they paid, and we both carried the tree out to

their van and started to fasten it to the top. Connor

was having a little difficulty getting his side secured,

so I came around to help once I finished with mine.

My arm brushed against his and I moved closer in.

Our sides touched. Scents of sap and sweat

dampened the otherwise warm encounter between

us.

"You have to knot it up here like this." I grunted and

flipped the twine around the ski rack, tying it off.

We both released and stepped back as we let out

breaths of air.

The family drove off and we waved. Once they were out of sight, Connor raised his hand in the air and turned to me. His breath was shallow and short. He was exhausted.

"Are you trying to give me a high-five?" I asked.

His hand fell from the air and to his side. His face went long, and he turned to go back into the lot. Catching up to his side, I laughed and pushed into him.

"You were joking, right?" I laughed.

He stopped and turned to me. Connor's face was so straight and serious. I thought he was seriously upset. "I wanted to high-five you, Angela."

"Oh . . ." I replied, not sure where to go from there.

He lurched forward and began laughing as hard as

he could.

I broke into a laugh and smacked him in the shoulder. "Jerk," I said, smiling and obviously joking. Connor was sneaking his way right into my heart. Without even realizing it, the feelings were developing. He was cutting his way in, uninvited but welcomed. Part of me was scared what it meant. The other part was excited. I liked him.

At the end of the day, we headed out to our cars. We were the only people left. Connor was back in his normal clothes, looking handsome as always. I found myself longing for a kiss. My lips almost ached for it by the time we made it out to the parking lot. Throughout the day, I found myself daydreaming of making out with him between customer arrivals. It wasn't like there were any cameras on the lot. I envisioned him kissing me delicately, then it growing to a passion that consumed me.

"I'm happy you came today." My eyes traced his coat up to his face, meeting his eyes.

He stepped closer and brushed a strand of hair out of my face, placing it behind my ear. Connor smiled and looked deeply into my eyes. "I thought about what you said last night as I went to sleep. I thought about you too. You were right. I need to make time for the important ones in my life. Plus, I love helping out for a good cause."

My heart raced as I could feel his warmth against my body. He was mere inches from me. He leaned in and kissed me on the cheek. It was disappointment in the form of a kiss, but in a weird way, I was happy.

"Come with me to Charlotte's."

"Right now?" he asked, taken aback.

I shook my head. "No. Next week."

"I can do it if it's after Tuesday. I'm going out of the country for work tomorrow for about a week, though I did enjoy a day off today." He grabbed my hand and brought it up to his lips. Kissing the top of it, he smiled up at me. "It was perfect."

"I enjoyed it also. We'll plan on that. I think it's on Wednesday or Thursday, so that works. I'll text you." We hugged and said our goodbyes. He went over to his car and I got into mine. Watching him for a moment through the driver side window, I recalled my text I had sent the other day about just being friends, and I could almost kick myself as regret

sank into my bones.

CHAPTER 8

Connor went out of the country for business, and I felt the days leading up to Charlotte's drag like molasses. I did keep somewhat busy working at the tree lot and spending time with Serenah, but Connor was on my mind *a lot*. Serenah had stumbled upon more Christmas decorations that had been left behind by Jody and Wayne in the garage, so we spent a few days alone just putting all that up and tossing away the stuff that was too old to use. The result was a Christmas wonderland, including Frosty and Santa Claus inflatables hanging out in the front yard. And though I had done well with keeping myself distracted, I couldn't help but wake up with a little extra energy to my step the morning Charlie, Serenah and I headed over to Charlotte's house, knowing I'd get to see Connor.

Arriving in the driveway of Charlotte's house, I saw two girls playing in the snow around an igloo through the back passenger window. It didn't look like much more than a mound of snow, but Charlie had told Serenah and me earlier in the morning about how they built it the same day they built the slide.

Getting out of the car, Charlie headed over to Dylan's house, which was next door. Serenah and I trekked through the snow over to the girls playing in the yard. Just as we came closer, the older girl went inside the igloo. Serenah called out to them as we came closer.

"Did Dylan make that for you girls?"

"Yep!" a little girl about the age of eight said with raised eyebrows that were tucked under a purple beanie cap. Getting down on all fours, she climbed into the igloo and then turned around inside, sticking her head out. "He said it's *my* princess fort until he can build me a *real* castle."

We came over to the igloo. Serenah got down on all fours while I hung back. *Where is he?* I wondered as I surveyed the entrance of the driveway. My pulse was racing with anticipation of seeing him again.

"Come check this out," Serenah said, pulling my attention to her and the igloo.

Getting on my knees, I looked inside the igloo. It was any kid's dream inside. Snow bricks lined the base of the inside and went up to form a dome at the top. I could tell these kids were loved.

The older girl, about ten, looked at us both as she stayed in the corner with her knees pulled up to her chest and furrowed eyebrows.

"What's wrong, Tristan?" Serenah asked.

"Bailey won't come play on the slide with me. She only wants to stay in the stupid snow house." She let out a grunt at the end of her sentence, and I almost laughed.

"Where's Emily?" Serenah asked, turning her head out from the opening of the igloo.

"Inside listening to music. *As always*," Tristan replied. "Ever since she started talking to that boy, she never wants to hang out. Ever."

"Hmm . . ." Serenah tapped her chin. "How about we go get Emily and go on the slide? I bet she'll come out if I ask."

Bailey, the younger one, scooted across the snow

and up to Serenah, grabbing onto her arm. "I don't like the slide," she whined. Her eyes widened. "I go too fast. Way too fast."

"Don't be a baby," Tristan said. "It's fun."

Pulling Bailey off her arm, Serenah backed out of the opening entirely and stood up. Hoisting Bailey up on her hip, she looked at Bailey and then at Tristan as she came out. "Let's go get Emily and go slide."

"She won't do it," Tristan warned. "She's a brat!"

"Hey, now. Don't call her that. Let's go see if we can talk her into coming with us."

Walking across the yard, I kept glancing toward the driveway. *Where's Connor?* continued to be my only thought as we traversed the yard over to the house.

Going inside, we found Emily sitting on the couch with ear buds in, listening to music. At our approach, she pulled them out and smiled at

Serenah. "Hey, Serenah."

"Come slide with your sisters," Serenah insisted.

"I don't want to go out there." Emily's eyes traveled across the living room and toward the back door through the kitchen. "It's too cold." She put her ear buds back in and went back to her music until Charlotte came into the living room from the kitchen. Walking over to the couch, Charlotte tapped Emily's shoulder. Emily promptly pulled the ear buds out.

"Emily Mae, get outside and have some fun in the snow with your sisters. It won't kill you."

"*Fine,* but I won't enjoy it." Getting up from the couch, she headed up the stairs but paused. Glancing back down at us all, she said, "I have to get dressed. It'll be a bit."

"Okay," Serenah said, and Emily darted up the rest

of the stairs.

"Sorry," Charlotte offered.

"It's fine," Serenah said. She came closer to her, and they hugged. Seeing the warmth of their relationship emanating from the expressions on their faces, I longed for such a girlfriend relationship. I had a friend like that at one point a few years back, before Ted passed—Sarah. After Ted was gone, though, her calls slowed and eventually stopped. My Christian counselor I saw for a bit after Ted's passing insisted it wasn't anything I did, but instead, it's just what often happens when couples are friends with other couples and one spouse is removed.

"You coming outside with us, Mommy?" Bailey asked as Serenah still had her on her hip.

Shaking her head, she smiled. "Smell that dinner cooking? I have to tend to it. Connor still coming?"

Serenah shrugged my direction as she looked over at me.

"I think so."

Charlotte nodded. "I haven't seen him in a while."

Serenah shook her head. "Neither have I. Lots of Katie and Joe, but only a couple of times for him. I heard he's been doing really good though."

"He seems like a nice guy," I offered as we all went through the kitchen and toward the back door.

"Don't limit yourself now, Angie." Charlotte touched my arm. "Did you get my message? I sent you my guy's Facebook page link."

Serenah laughed. "*My guy?* What if Dylan heard you talking like that?"

"Oh, shut it! He's not *my* guy. I just forgot his name for a minute. Michael. His name is Michael."

Charlotte nodded confidently, though her face was

flushed in embarrassment.

Letting out a short laugh, I nodded. "I haven't gotten ahold of him, but I saw it."

"She went out with *Connor* and had a blast, *then* he surprised her and worked a day at the tree lot with her. Super cute," Serenah said as she looked over at me with a raised brow and a grin. "She has the hots for him."

Slapping her shoulder, I shook my head as I blushed. "It's not *super* serious."

"Uh-huh. All week, you kept telling me cute little things he did during your date and day working together. You seem pretty hung up on him." Charlotte's eyebrows went up. "Sounds pretty serious."

Shrugging a shoulder, I said, "I don't think so. I haven't heard much from him."

"Get ahold of Michael." Charlotte nodded as she grabbed the handle of the back door and opened it for us.

We all went outside while Charlotte stayed back to continue cooking. As we approached the slide that the guys had made along the side of the house, I noticed the serene quiet that was present. Surveying the slide, I was impressed by the extensiveness that the guys had gone through in building it. At least a half-acre in length, the slide was more like a course for the Olympic luge with all the slopes and turns it had. A mound of snow and ice with built-in stairs was the starting point of the slide. Bailey's hesitation to go down it made a lot more sense seeing it in person. The course ran all the way down to near the shoreline of the lake. With raised eyebrows, I shook my head as I marveled.

"Wow . . ."

"You're *that* surprised I showed up?" Connor said, coming up to my side.

Startled, I turned to him. "Hey, stranger."

He smiled as our eyes connected. I was glad he finally showed.

"Glad you could make it," Serenah said, pulling his attention away from me.

Connor rubbed his hands together to gain warmth and nodded down toward her. "Hello again, Serenah. It's been a while."

Leaning into Connor's ear, I said, "We're going to have some chili in a bit if you want to stay."

"That sounds good." Leaning in closer, he said, "Sorry about not being much for words the last week. With the time change and sketchy cell service—"

"It's okay."

Charlie and Dylan came trekking over in the snow as Tristan headed to the slide. Charlie spotted Connor and came right over to us. "Hey, man. Long time, no see. Missed you last month."

They exchanged a firm handshake. "Work's been crazy with the holidays," Connor said with a smile on his face.

My contact started to bother me, so I excused myself and went inside. Charlotte directed me to the bathroom upstairs since the one downstairs was out of order due to a burst pipe that froze outside due to the ridiculously below average nights we had been having for several consecutive days.

As I came out of the bathroom upstairs, I could hear a faint cry coming from the direction of a room. *Emily?* I wondered, walking over to the partially opened door. I almost left it alone, but something inside drew me to knock, so I did.

Knock, knock.

After a few light knocks, I pushed the door open a fraction and looked inside.

She looked up from her phone and pulled out her ear buds and wiped her face of tears. "What do you want?" she said with a glare.

"Just want to make sure you're okay. Sorry. I shouldn't—" With my hand on the doorknob, I starting closing it when she spoke.

"Stupid boyfriend drama." Looking, I saw her glaring out the window as another tear escaped her eye and ran down her cheek.

Pushing the door all the way open, I went inside.

"What happened?"

"I don't want to talk about it." Emily's eyes drifted

over to me as I sat down on the bed. "Was high school hard for you? With guys?"

I laughed. "Unbelievably hard."

She sat up more on the bed and leaned forward as she crossed her legs. "Really? You're so pretty though."

Smiling, I said, "Sure. But I didn't know that."

Looking her in the eyes, I said, "You're beautiful, Emily. Don't let any lame boy make you feel otherwise."

Her chin dipped as she played with the headphone cord. Peering up at me, she said, "I feel like I'm never going to graduate and I'm going to be single forever."

Turning more on the bed toward her, I brought a leg up and under me. "It's going to get better. High school is nothing compared to the real world. Just focus on your grades and having fun with your friends, and don't worry about boys. It'll be over before you know it."

"I'll try."

Standing up, I turned and looked at her. "You'll be out of the house and doing your own thing soon enough. Don't miss out on the things that really matter in the long run." Not asking her to come outside like she told everybody she would, I left it at that and headed back downstairs.

Back outside, I joined Connor's side while all the adults chatted. Then, after about ten minutes, Emily came out.

Bundled up with a scarf and snow gear, she smiled over at me as she made her way through the snow up to the slide. Connor spotted it. Leaning into my ear, he said, "I heard Dylan talking about how she wouldn't come out earlier. What'd you do?"

Smiling as I kept my eyes on Emily, I said, "I just talked to her."

Nodding slowly, he raised an eyebrow and relaxed into his stance.

"You're going to love it," Dylan insisted as he headed toward the starting point right behind Emily. "Keep your hands inside and use your body to control the sled."

"Okay," she replied, climbing to the top of the mound. Part fear and part annoyance could be seen in Emily's eyes as she surveyed the course. Adjusting the sled, Dylan helped hold it steady as she sat down. He backed up and she scooted to the edge.

Whoosh!

Screaming and laughing as she flew down the slide, she took every corner beaming with a grin. At the bottom of the slide, she rolled off the sled after it came to a stop. Jumping up, she said, "That was awesome!" Smiling, she hurried through the snow to go again, but Tristan stopped her with a hand extended.

"Let me try, let me try."

Glancing over at the other adults, I saw Charlie with his arm around Serenah. Looking to my other side, I saw Connor and our eyes connected. He put his arm around my shoulder, and I felt my heart flutter as I let myself come in closer to him. *I could get used to this.*

After our meal that evening, I was feeling the need for a breath of fresh air. Going outside on her back porch, I gazed up at the stars. A few moments later, Connor joined me.

"Thought you might like something that will warm you up," he said, handing me a cup of coffee.

"Thank you." Taking the warm mug from him, I took a drink. "Yummy. Peppermint."

"I knew you liked it because of the airport in Seattle." My heart fluttered at his words. Adjusting his footing, he said, "I've been thinking of you a lot the last week."

"Really? I've been thinking about you too."

Connor took a step toward me. I could feel his warmth against my body. Framing my face in his palms, he looked at me, looked at me like I was his, and then he kissed me. His warm lips gently pressed against mine, sending tidal waves of warmth through my body. He paused and pulled back.

"Would you like to come with me to a company holiday dinner? It's in a couple of days." His cheeks were red from the cold, but his eyes were set on mine.

"I'd love to, Connor." Leaning back into him, I kissed him and smiled.

He broke into a wide grin. "Thank you," he said, and then we kissed again.

CHAPTER 9

Buying a dress for the dinner party might have been

odd for just *anyone* who was going, but I was the

date of the owner of the company—not *just* anyone.

It made me feel special. This dress, in addition to

smiling and being sociable, would be the ticket to

making Connor glad to let my arm intertwine with

his for the evening. I wanted to make him happy.

It was late afternoon, and he'd be here any moment.

Still tucked away in my bathroom, I curled the last

few strands of hair. The curls of blonde, the right

amount of makeup, and the absolutely stunning

crimson red over-one-shoulder formal dress all came

together in a perfect trifecta. Seeing myself looking back in the mirror, I smiled. I looked happy. I felt pretty. That looming darkness that had been present off and on for years wasn't there this time.

The doorbell rang, and my stomach flipped. *That's gotta be him,* I thought to myself as I turned and heard shuffled footsteps over to the door. Leaving the bathroom, I grabbed my black purse from the bed and headed upstairs.

I arrived in the living room, and Connor's eyes fell onto me mid-conversation with Charlie and words stopped. His mouth dropped open and his eyes went wide. He was mesmerized. My heart fluttered deep inside me as I filled with streams of happiness throughout.

He came over to me and bent a knee slightly as he dropped his head and kissed the top of my hand.

"My lady, you look absolutely gorgeous this night."

I laughed and shooed him away. He looked quite handsome in his black suit and red tie that had Christmas trees on it. Serenah walked into the room from the dining area. She came right up beside Charlie. Something on her face seemed different. Not good, not bad, just different. Charlie put his arm around her back and they both smiled at us.

"What's going on?" My eyes trained on Serenah. She turned and looked up at Charlie beside her.

"We're having a baby!"

Hurrying across the room as much as I could in a dress, I wrapped my arms tightly around Serenah and hugged her, congratulating her as I did so. Connor gave a congratulatory pat on Charlie's shoulder and they started talking.

Pulling Serenah to the side, I gently put my hand on

her arm and asked in a whisper, "You okay?"

Her eyes glistened as we both thought of Hope. "It makes me think of *her*."

I nodded. "Isaiah 57:1 says, 'the righteous are taken away to be spared from evil.' Who knows what could have happened if you had Hope, Serenah. If John showed up and you had Hope . . . you just don't know what could have happened. Your entire life could be different." Giving her a hug, I said, "It's going to be okay."

"I know." A sniffle and a nod came from her as we broke our embrace. She dabbed her eyes with her palm to get the tears away. "Though I seem sad, I'm quite excited." Connor and Charlie came over to us, and Charlie slipped his hand to Serenah's lower back.

"We were trying to wait until Christmas," Charlie

said, shaking his head as he smiled. "But we couldn't. We were too excited to break the news."

"I'm so happy for you two."

Arriving at the Lincoln Center, Connor got out and opened my door for me. As I stepped out, he pulled me in close to him. Surprised, I smiled as our lips touched. Melting at the gentle touch of his lips against mine, I felt warmth radiating in my chest. Pulling back gently, he smiled at me.

"I know I already said it, but you look absolutely gorgeous, Angela. I'm going to have my work cut out for me keeping the other guys away from you tonight." Connor grinned as he stuck out his arm to me and I grabbed on.

We walked across the street and up to the doors of the Lincoln Center. A doorman took our jackets, and we walked down the hallway to a big open room. The room had streams of white and red fabric that hung from one side of the tall ceiling to the other, and snowflakes dangled in the air above our heads like stars in the sky. There were a dozen and a half tables, a dance floor, and a DJ station.

The only people there when we showed up were a few staffers who were catering the event. Nobody else had shown up as early as we did. Connor led me to a table and then headed over to a doorway that led into the kitchen. I waited.

He came back out five minutes later with a chef and walked over to me. "Elnardo, this is Angie."

"Oh, yes. She is *very* pretty." His voice had a thick accent, and he went for my hand, but Connor shooed him away.

"*Hey now,* Elnardo." Connor was light and playful, but there was a hint of seriousness in his tone toward the man.

The Chef let out a hearty laugh and nodded to Connor. "I must get back in my kitchen to finish preparing. You pay me too much to not get back in there." He looked at me. "It was nice to meet you, Angie."

Connor sat down in the chair near me and scooted it closer to me. He took one of my hands into his and rubbed the top of it. "Elnardo is an old friend of mine. He's one of the best cooks in Spokane. Voted number twelve in the Northwest last year. He is a good man. You okay?"

Smiling, I nodded. "I'm fine, Connor. He seems nice, and I love that accent."

He laughed. "The accent is a perk."

"I notice you call me Angela but introduce me as Angie to others. How come?"

"I think Angela is a beautiful name for a beautiful woman, but I know you prefer Angie, so others can call you that. But to me, you'll always be Angela."

The way he said *Angela* right in that moment caused a flutter in my chest to pulse through me.

People showed up within the hour, and soon, the entire place was hopping with music, conversation and dancing. Connor didn't have any champagne with his staff. I thought it was because of the whole nature of their relationship, but I found out that wasn't the case when I offered him a drink from my glass. He pulled me aside, away from the crowd, and told me about his past experiences with insomnia and how bad the drinking had gotten.

"I'm sorry. I wouldn't have if I had known." My head hung.

"No, don't apologize." He came in closer, lifting my chin with the side of his finger. Smiling at me, he shook his head. "You didn't know. It's all right."

"This champagne is kind of killing my head anyway. I haven't had a glass of alcohol in like a year." I set the glass down on the table in the hall, and he came up behind me and wrapped his arms around me. I smiled, letting my head fall back onto his shoulder.

"Kind of nice to get away from the crowd." His voice was but a sweet whisper in my ear. He kissed my earlobe lightly, then just below my ear on my neck, sending shivers through me.

"You sure seem to be liked by everyone who works for you." He pulled my hair back and played with it a little. He let out a short laugh.

"You know how that is . . . they get paid to like you."

Bringing all my hair over one shoulder, he lowered

his lips to the back of my neck and kissed. I closed

my eyes and let myself focus on that feeling—that

feeling of being alive and overtaken with happiness,

and that feeling of the rest of the world

disappearing.

"Angela . . ." His voice was soft, his tone smooth and

sending me deeper into the warmth of his arms

around me.

"Yeah?" My head still rested on his shoulder, and I

glanced up at him.

Suddenly, a couple came barreling out from the

banquet room. We separated immediately as we

were jolted from our moment. The woman was in

hysterics, mascara running, and her date tried to

comfort her, but she pulled away and headed down

the hallway toward the exit.

"What's going on, Jonathan?" Connor asked, prompting the man to come over to us.

Jonathan shook his head. It was apparent he was trying to hold back tears as his eyes glistened with a glaze. "Marie's brother was just shot. He's a cop in Atlanta."

"No," Connor said, glancing toward the exit. He stepped closer to Jonathan and touched his arm. "Is he alive?"

"It's not looking good. He's in ICU."

Shaking his head, Connor looked back at me and raised a hand. "Come here. Let's all pray." I came up to him. Putting his arms around Jonathan and me, Connor led us in a prayer. "God, we come to You today, pleading for You to help Marie's brother . . ."

Jonathan added, "Frank."

Connor continued, "Please Lord, we lift Frank up into Your hands. Help him heal, help him live. Watch over his unit, and we pray that You just wrap your arms around this family at this time. Amen."

Lifting our heads, Connor and Jonathan were both in tears. My eyes were welling with tears. Connor turned to Jonathan and grabbed his shoulder in a comforting way. "Tell Marie I'll have my assistant book the first flight out for you two. She'll need your support."

"You don't have—"

Connor shook his head. "I won't take no for an answer. If she refuses, tell her I'll fire her if she doesn't get on that plane and go. And also tell her not to worry about the time she misses at work."

Jonathan smiled and more tears came. He hugged Connor tightly and then hurried down the hallway to the exit. Connor came back over to me, our moment far beyond gone. I felt drained. He took my hand and kissed it. "That's so sad . . ."

I nodded, watching the exit door close. Turning my eyes to Connor, I saw how genuine of a person he was. He really cared. "I don't understand how people can just take a life like that."

"What do you mean?" Connor asked.

"To have so little care for human life. I don't understand it."

He nodded. "It's sad."

Putting my arms around his neck, I looked at Connor. "What were you going to ask me?"

He shrugged. "I don't remember." Letting out a breath of air, his eyes glanced back toward the doorway of the banquet hall. "We should get back in there."

CHAPTER 10

After the company party that night, I dreamed of Connor. The next night too. He was consuming my thoughts, and worry began to creep into me. He was becoming too important too quickly, and the reality was that I was going to go back to Florida after Christmas and we would be separated.

Two days after the company Christmas party, while I was sitting on my bed in the early afternoon reading my Bible, I came across a passage of verses that had been highlighted by Ted. Streaks of yellow highlighted Ephesians 2:3-6.

3 All of us also lived among them at one time, gratifying the cravings of our flesh and following its desires and thoughts. Like the rest, we were by nature deserving of wrath. 4 But because of his great love for us, God, who is rich in mercy, 5 made us alive with Christ even when we were dead in transgressions—it is by grace you have been saved.

The passage itself, as a whole, did not catch my attention right away, but that word I loathed, *dead*, triggered the realization that the anniversary of Ted's death had come and gone without so much as a thought on my part. *It was last Tuesday,* I thought to myself as tears welled in my eyes. *How could I forget?* Guilt rattled my core as I rested my hands on my open Bible. Glancing down at the Scriptures, I read it over again. This time, a different part jumped out at me. *Gratifying the cravings of our flesh and following its desires and thoughts.* The verse only worsened my sadness and made me feel like the most selfish widow on earth.

Serenah came through the open door and saw me crying. "What's wrong?" she asked.

"I missed it."

Confused, she came over to the bed and sat down. "Missed what?"

"He died four years ago . . . last Tuesday."

Reaching over, Serenah grabbed my hand and caressed the top with her thumb. "It's okay, Angie."

Pursed lips formed a thin line across my face as I shook my head. Tears continued to pour out of me as grief consumed my being. "It's not okay, Serenah. I *never* forget the date. I was too busy enjoying my life and thinking about Connor. And I forgot all about Ted!"

Standing up from the bed, she came closer and gave me a hug. It did little to comfort me. While I had been busy thinking and dreaming of Connor, and even kissing him, Ted's passing wasn't remembered. A pit began to form in my stomach.

Throughout the entirety of the day, I wept every time I thought not only of Ted, but of Connor. My heart was weighing down with remorse and grief over forgetting the day that had lived for so long as a stinging reminder of the worst day of my life. I also couldn't help having a feeling of guilt. I had enjoyed my time with Connor, and that truth made the circumstances all the worse. My heart had enjoyed another man's company.

After Charlie and Serenah retired to their private quarters for the evening, I stayed up a little longer in the living room. The shimmering tinsel on the tree reflected the Christmas lights Charlie had hung beautifully. The ornaments, which Serenah had strategically placed, brought the tree to life. Then there, on the side facing the windows, hung the ornament that Connor had given me. Earlier in the day, I went to grab it and throw it away, but Serenah stopped me. She insisted that it stay.

Taking a drink of my cider, I found the bottom of the coffee mug, so I stood up and went into the kitchen to place it in the sink. As I crossed into the kitchen, I saw a picture of Charlie and Serenah on the fridge. They were smiling and happy. I thought of Ted. *We were happy once,* I thought to myself.

Before he went off and died. Continuing over to the sink, I ran water in the cup, rinsing it out, and then I set it in the sink. Hearing a noise behind me, I turned.

"Just getting a drink of water. Don't mind me," Emma said as she moved with grunts and apparent pain in every step across the kitchen floor. Stepping out of the way, I leaned against the counter. She ran the faucet and then opened the cupboard.

"Emma?" I said gently as I recalled from previous conversations with Serenah that she had been married before.

"Yes?"

Seeing the clock focus in behind her head of gray hair, I saw it was after eleven. *She's probably too tired to chat,* I thought. "Never mind. It's too late."

Taking a drink of the water, she set the glass down

on the counter beside the sink for later use. Raising her eyebrows, she looked steadily at me. "It's never too late for a question. What's on your mind?"

"How old were you when your husband passed? What can you tell me about it that you learned? I'm struggling." My eyes pleaded for her to open up and spill her heart to me. I needed relief of this knotting pain in my stomach and in my heart.

A smile broke across her face as she looked up at the ceiling. "Don't confuse my smiling for thinking I'm happy he's dead. It's the memories I love. Let's see now. I was forty-two. Oh, dear. To be that young again." She made eye contact with me and rested a hand on the island countertop as she shook her head at me. "Loss is never easy, my dear. It's one of the few things I've come in contact with that truly changes a person for good."

"You never got over it?" I asked.

Swaying her head back and forth slightly, she let go of the counter and raised her eyebrows. "Not *fully,* but I hate to even say that." She came up to me and placed a hand on my shoulder. "It's not about *moving on.* It's about learning to continue living when you don't want to anymore. It's also learning to love life even though that person isn't here. You have to give yourself permission to do that. The hardest part of losing a spouse for me was allowing myself to get to a place where I could be happy again, a place where I didn't feel guilty about being happy. Then, over time, and everyone is different, when you think of your love, you're happy you have the memory instead of sad they're not here anymore. It's the process of letting go but not forgetting."

Her words dripped with honey and filled me with joy. Tears streamed down my cheeks. "I don't know why I'm crying, but you just seem to get it!" I wiped my tears from my face and sniffed.

Letting her hand return to her side, she sighed and her shoulders slumped. Shaking her head, she looked down for a moment and then directly at me. "It's a sad thing to understand, but yes, I do understand. You have to let your heart beat again, Angie. You have to let yourself find happiness and joy."

Nodding, I said, "I've done okay for a while. Then recently, I forgot the anniversary of his death."

Emma tapped her chin and had the most serious look on her face. "I wonder what *he* would think about that."

"What?" I asked, shaking my head in confusion.

She smiled. "He's not going to care you forgot, Angie. He's dancing with Jesus." Framing my cheek in her aged hand, she looked me in the eyes. "You can be happy. If you need the permission, this is me granting it to you." Releasing my face, she turned and saw the time. "I'd better get back to bed."

"Thank you, Emma."

She coughed and nodded as she took her leave from the kitchen. As she left, I repeated all she had said, and one part, specifically, strummed a deep part of my soul. *Let my heart beat again.* It was getting late, so I headed downstairs to my room and got ready for bed. As I got under the covers, I received a message from Peter asking to hang out. *Not tonight, hot youth pastor guy. I'm too tired.* Ignoring it, I rolled over and went to bed.

CHAPTER 11

Connor hadn't texted or communicated with me since our evening together at his company Christmas party four days ago, and I was okay with that. I didn't text him either. I realized how much I had already fallen for him by the dreams and constant thinking of him, and I was happy to have some distance.

Bone-chilling gusts were swooping through the tree lot that morning, and even though I had packed on an extra sweatshirt under my coat, the protection did little for my face. Each gust nipped at my face and kept my cheeks permanently rose colored as I worked through the morning helping customers haul trees out to their cars. My little helper, Micah, wasn't there that morning either. He was at school. In between customers, all I could think about was when Connor helped me that one day, the ridiculous outfit of Don's he wore and the way he showed up out of nowhere. Part of me hoped he'd just show up again, even though I was trying to give myself and my thoughts space from that. As the eleven o'clock hour rolled around, I had just finished loading a tree atop a van full of children who wouldn't stop running around the lot as Mommy and Daddy couldn't decide which tree to get. Taking the five-dollar tip they had given me over to the cash register, I dropped it in the cup when a man approached through the entrance.

"What's a cute gal like you doing working in a place

like this?" the guy asked.

"If you're attempting to hit on me, you're doing a horrible job." Turning around, I left and went to find another customer. He followed behind me down one of the rows of trees.

"C'mon. It was a compliment," he said. "I need a tree."

Stopping, I turned around and glared at him. "I'm covered in sap, smell like a pine tree, and have been out in the freezing cold for hours now. I'm sorry, but I'm not in the mood to get hit on by some creep."

Seeing his wedding ring on, I shook my head.

"Gross. A married man at that!"

Don came up beside me and lifted his chin to the man. "Best get out of here."

"I need a *tree*."

"What you *need* is a good butt kicking. Now get."

Don took a step toward the man, and before he could take another, the guy backed away and left. Turning, he said, "Why don't you take a break and go get yourself a cup of coffee? Maybe it'll warm up your attitude too."

"But that—" Don's look alone cut through me. I knew I had been walking around annoyed that morning, so I flushed with embarrassment and nodded. Tears welled in my eyes, and I headed for the exit. Crossing the parking lot, I pulled out my phone and called Connor. I wanted to talk to him. It went straight to voice mail.

"Ugh!" I shouted as I hung up. *You're obsessed with Connor, just admit it.* The thought freaked me out, but I knew it was true. One night when I was going to sleep, I thought about him until one o'clock in the morning. I even went upstairs just to look at the ornament on the tree.

If I didn't want to be fixated on Connor and wanted to be able to leave this place with my heart still intact, I needed a distraction, maybe a date with someone else. Convincing myself, I brought up the message from Peter and replied back to him.

Me: Sure. I'm free tonight.

The warmth inside the grocery store helped thaw the gnawing coldness that seemed to be part of every shift at the tree lot the deeper we got into winter. Seeing a couple of kids take a sample from a bakery worker who was handing out bits of Christmas cookies, I decided to partake. Smiling at the young woman, who couldn't have been a day over eighteen, I thought about what it was like to be that young again. The lack of bills to pay made for a

different life altogether. Nibbling on the partial
cookie, I walked over to the coffee stand that sat on
the opposite side of the store. Ordering a house
coffee, I took the welcomed piping hot cup and sat
down at one of the tables in the coffee area.

My phone buzzed.

It was Peter.

**Peter: Awesome. Send me your address and I'll
pick you up at six, if that works for you.**

I replied back with the address to the inn. Peter
could help take my mind off Connor and maybe I
could have some fun. It's not like any of it really
mattered. I didn't live in Spokane or out at the inn
and I would soon be leaving.

Peter showed up on time, and that was about the best part of the date. Minutes into the meal, I was beyond annoyed. He was a sweet guy who did amazing things for the greater good of his local congregation and the kids he pastored, but he never stopped talking. He drummed on and on about this project and that project. And while I was a huge advocate of being the hands and feet of Christ, there was another aspect I felt needed to accompany all those actions—humility. As he talked more about a homeless outreach program after I tried to send the visual cues I wasn't interested, my eyes and mind wandered away from the table. While taking in the breathtakingly gorgeous woodwork of the pillars and archways inside The Old Spaghetti Factory, I thought of Connor. *Did I scare him off somehow?* I wondered.

". . . Angie?" Peter asked, but I only caught the last part because he used my name.

"I'm sorry, what?" I shook my head and directed my attention to him.

He flashed me a crooked smile and let out a sarcastic laugh. Setting down his napkin on the table, he crossed his arms. "Did you hear *anything* I said? I feel like I keep losing you."

My heart pounded in my ears. I didn't want to be here. It felt like a mistake. It didn't help that he was boring and only spoke of himself. "I'm sorry. You're just talking a lot."

He nodded, but his lips were pursed. "*Fine.* Let's talk about you. What's your deal? Why are you single? You're divorced, aren't you?"

"Nope. My husband's dead," I replied.

"Oh . . ." His tone shifted dramatically and his shoulders relaxed as his arms uncrossed. "I'm sorry. I didn't know that."

Standing up, I slid my purse's strap up onto my shoulder and shrugged. "How would you? This is the most I've spoken tonight, and it's all been about you. Let's just pretend this didn't happen and part ways."

Taking my leave, I headed out of the restaurant right after the bread sticks but before the entree. I didn't have time for a person like him. I'd find a movie to go to by myself. I didn't need a jerk to accompany me the rest of the evening. On my way out the door, I called for a cab to pick me up.

Walking out of the theater and down the slope to the sidewalk, I about fell over when I saw Connor across the street. Standing there a moment longer, I squinted to make sure it was really him—it was.

"Connor!" I shouted.

He couldn't hear me over the sounds of the cars zipping by, nor did he see me. Raising my hand, I called out to him again as I came to the curb. Once clear, I crossed the street over to him.

His eyebrows shot up at the sight of me and I smiled at him on my approach.

"Angie," he said. His hands were deep in his long black coat and he was wearing a black turtleneck. "What are you doing here?"

"I was just at a movie. You know, I tried calling you earlier and even texted you." I was confused as he never called me Angie.

Suddenly, a woman came out of the coffee shop behind him and handed him a cup.

Raising an eyebrow, I looked at her.

"This is Natalie." Connor looked over at the woman and said, "This is Angie. She's a friend of mine from Florida visiting for a bit."

"Oh, wow. I bet it's like *really* hot there, huh? And it's *really* cold here."

Who is this woman? I thought to myself. "Like, totally," I replied to her, matching her dumb tone as I grinned over at Connor, searching his eyes for an explanation. He smiled but didn't say a word.

"We've gotta go, but it was so nice meeting you, Hon," the woman said, linking arms with Connor as she caught our exchanged looks.

"I was just on a date earlier," I added, trying to make myself feel relevant, maybe even attempting to make him care a little.

"Oh?" Connor said with a suspicious tone.

"He was being dumb though, so I ditched him and came to a movie by myself."

The blonde ditsy girl pulled on Connor's coat. "We should get walking so we stay warm."

Connor nodded to her and then said to me, "Have a good night, Angie."

"You too." Turning, they both left down the sidewalk. Watching as they walked away from where I was standing, I pulled out my cellphone and called for a cab. I felt like a complete idiot, not just for the way I tried to brag about my bad date, but for ever investing in so many emotions and thoughts of Connor. He said it best when he introduced me as 'a friend who's visiting from Florida.'

After getting back to the inn that evening, I changed into my pajamas and got ready for bed. Rubbing lotion into my hands and up my arms, I heard my phone buzz on the nightstand. A dollop of hope surfaced in my heart. *Connor?* Leaning over, I turned the phone over to see it who it was. Peter thanked me for an amazing night, followed by a few laughing faces. Rolling my eyes, I went back to applying my lotion.

CHAPTER 12

Sitting on a stool in the kitchen, I enjoyed a bagel and cream cheese the next morning while I read the comics in the newspaper. Serenah was already busy with cleaning the kitchen. She knew I had a date last night with Peter, but neither of us brought it up. Wiping the same part of the counter for the fifth time in ten minutes, I set the paper down and looked at her.

"Go ahead. Ask."

Turning, she tossed the rag into the sink and leaned her arms across the island countertop. "Do tell," she said, leaning into the palms of her hands as they held her smile up.

Ding, Dong

Her eyes rolled toward the entryway at the sound of the doorbell. Standing upright, she looked back at me narrowly as she began heading out of the kitchen. "This isn't over."

I laughed and turned back to my newspaper. Paying no attention to the conversation going on at the front door, I continued with my comics until a few minutes later when Serenah returned. Peering up from the paper, I saw not only her but Connor. My heart slammed against my ribcage and I suddenly became aware of my 'just got out of bed' look I was sporting with pajamas and unkempt hair. Setting the paper down, I stood up from the stool at the island and took a step back.

"What are you doing here, Connor?"

He came around the island in the kitchen and touched the side of my arm as he led me down into the dining area. "We need to talk."

Four words nobody ever wants to hear.

Serenah nodded from the kitchen and took off down the hallway to her private quarters. Connor turned his head and saw her leave and then turned back to me. Feeling a mixture of vulnerability and surprise, my pulse raced. "What's going on?"

Wringing his hands, his lips parted for a second like he was going to speak. Looking into his eyes, I caught a glimpse of a world I didn't understand behind them. Red outlines around bloodshot eyes indicated that something was definitely amiss. "Can we sit?"

"By all means," I replied, holding out a hand to a table nearby. We both took a seat and he scooted the chair in closer to the table. Bringing his hands together atop the table, he dipped his chin to his chest. Whatever this was, it was serious.

"Is it about that girl?" I asked.

"No." He laughed a little as he shook his head. "That girl was nothing. No, I need to tell you something about my past."

"What is it?" I asked, leaning in as he leaned in more.

His head swayed to the left and then to the right. "There's no way to really say it other than to just say it. It's kind of the reason why I haven't been talking to you a whole lot lately. I don't know if you've noticed that."

"Ha. Yeah . . . I've noticed."

He nodded. "I had hoped dodging calls and texts and just not seeing you before you left would let this die down between us, but seeing you last night tore me to pieces. I was so jealous you had been on a date with someone else even if it was terrible. Anyways, there's something you need to know. Remember how I told you I dealt with an episode of depression?"

I nodded slowly, trying to anticipate what he would say.

"Well, I tried to kill myself." Pulling up his sleeves, he showed me his arms.

My insides tightened around my heart. My heart broke for him. He began weeping and trying to hide it with his hands as his chin held tightly against his chest. I reached across the table to touch his hands. "Connor . . ."

He wiped his eyes hard and then looked at me. "No. I don't want you to feel bad for me, Angie." He stood up. "You probably think I'm just selfish. It's why we would never work."

Shaking my head with confusion, I said, "Why would I think that?"

He walked past me and over to the doors that led out to the lake. Staring out, he shook his head. "How could you *not*? Your husband *died*, by no choice of his own." Connor turned around and came over to me at the table. Bending at the knees, he looked into my eyes with his sad, red, swollen eyes. "I tried to take *my own life*, Angie."

Framing his face with my hands as my heart almost bled through my pajamas, I shook my head and tears started rolling down my cheeks. "Connor, I've been there. Do you know how many times I felt like giving up right after I lost Ted? I understand how it gets to that point."

"You got to that point because your husband died. I was there because I am selfish and weak. You said at the company party that you don't understand how someone can take a life. Well, that's what I tried to do. Look, you leave in a couple of weeks to go back home, and then we'll never see each other again. I think we need to leave it be and not see each other anymore."

Serenah walked back into the kitchen and we both looked over at her. She took a step back toward the hallway, but Connor shook his head.

"I should go," Connor said. His unease with Serenah nearby was apparent.

I grabbed his arm to stop him. He looked at me.

"Don't go. Let's talk more," I pleaded.

"I don't want to talk." He shrugged my hand off his arm and left, cutting through the living room and through the foyer to the front door.

The door closed, and Serenah came into the dining room and shook her head as she surveyed my tear-soaked face. "What happened?" she asked as she touched both my shoulders.

Letting out a cry, I let my face fall into her shoulder. "He told me about his attempted suicide."

Serenah gently patted my head as I continued to cry. "He recommitted his life to the Lord and has made marvelous changes in his life since then. Do you want me to call in for you down at the tree lot? It's only volunteer work. You don't *have* to go."

Shaking my head, I wiped my eyes and said, "I really need the distraction today. I'll go get ready."

Serenah stopped me before I left the room. "It's clear he likes you, Angie. Maybe he just needs to come to terms with things before he fully admits that."

The truth was that I didn't want to talk either. My mind felt clouded, my thoughts jumbled. I simply nodded at Serenah and continued downstairs.

That evening, the town of Newport had their annual Christmas tree lighting ceremony on Main Street and everyone was in attendance. Stations with free hot cocoa were all over in the street, and the tree, which replaced the location of an iron horse for the holidays, according to Serenah, was ready to have its lights turned on. Don down at the tree lot told me earlier that day that it took twelve Boy Scouts, three ladders, and half a day of stringing lights to cover the whole thirty-foot tree in lights.

Snow began to fall lightly as the final five minutes

until the tree lighting approached. All of Serenah and Charlie's friends were there, even Connor. Just having him there, even though we weren't talking, brought a certain level of comfort to me. The way he made me feel by merely being present was indefinable. Sadness also clouded my thoughts though. *We could've been great if he'd just let us be. Distance wouldn't matter.* "You should try to be less obvious." Katie grinned at me as she raised an eyebrow and shot a quick look Connor's way.

"What? Sorry."

"I'm just *playing*. You really like him, don't you?" Taking a sip of her cocoa, she continued, "He's a good guy, Angie."

"Yeah. Not like that Peter guy."

"Hey, I didn't know him that well. I just figured since he was a youth pastor, he'd be okay." Katie shrugged. "Sorry."

"It's okay." Glancing over at Connor again, I said, "Do you know why he is trying to keep himself distanced from me?" Looking over at her as I realized I was bringing her in the middle, I shook my head as my eyebrows went up. "I'm sorry. I don't mean to bring you into it."

Katie peered over at Connor. "It's okay to ask. Honestly? I think he doesn't feel he deserves you. You lost someone while he attempted to end his own life. That and you're leaving to go back to Florida in two weeks."

"What?" I replied, taken aback. "*Deserves* me? What's that even mean?"

"Connor feels a lot of guilt over what he's done in his life. Even with Christ as his Savior, Connor hasn't been able to get over some of the guilt associated with all the junk. Don't tell him I told you any of that. Just food for thought."

"Angie," Micah, the kid from the tree lot, said gleefully as he tugged on my coat. Turning to him, I smiled at him.

"What is it, Micah?" Our breaths rose up from our lips as we spoke.

"Don's letting me flip the switch!" He grinned from ear to ear at his own words.

Letting my mouth drop open in an over-reactive response, I said, "No way! You lucky duck!"

His eyes went wide, and the little boy nodded frantically. "Watch me do it, Angie! Watch me." He scurried over to the tree and up to Don's side as I stood back upright. Watching him with a grin, I gave him a thumbs-up when his eyes found mine a moment later. The scores of people that were there that night with cups of cocoa in hand all turned their attention to the tree and Don as his voice came over the microphone system and speaker.

"Thanks, everybody, for coming out. It's a bit cold out here right now, so let's not waste any time."

The crowd laughed.

"Three . . . two . . . one!"

An array of colors lit up the Christmas tree in a grand display of beauty. Glancing over toward Connor, I saw him stuck in a wondrous gaze at the tree and I thought about what Katie had told me about him. *He doesn't feel like he deserves me?* I thought. *Is it that or that I'm going back to Florida in a week and a half?*

CHAPTER 13

Though it hurt to think that Connor wasn't willing to see if we had something more, I spent the rest of my visit enjoying time with Serenah. We baked, we sewed stockings, and we reminisced about childhood memories. We found a great deal on red poinsettias at the grocery store and used them to help put the finishing touches on the inn. On Christmas Eve, Serenah sent me down to the grocery store to pick up a can of baked beans because of Nathan's love of them. He was one of her and Charlie's friends that was coming over that night. Intently looking over the million variations of baked beans in the canned goods aisle of the grocery store, I didn't know which brand to get. Christmas music rang in my ears as I looked over the rather large selection of beans. It was the only store in Newport still open at four o'clock on Christmas Eve. *I've heard of Bush's baked beans. I wonder if that's what I'm supposed to get. I'll call her.* Pulling out my phone from my purse, I called Serenah and asked about the beans. As I was standing idle, an unexpected visitor turned down my aisle.

It was Connor.

"Oh, no . . ."

"What?" Serenah asked, her tone worried.

Turning sharply away from Connor, I lowered my voice. "Connor is here!"

"*Well* . . . you know he's coming tonight."

"What? Really?"

"Bush's Baked Beans Traditional is fine! Go talk to him."

Click.

Lowering my phone from my ear, I felt my insides freeze over as I turned around. He was reading the label on a can of corn and hadn't noticed me standing in the aisle yet. Glancing down the opposite way, I entertained the thought of running away like a coward. *That'd look ridiculous,* I thought. Turning, I faced him. My pulse soared and anxiety knotted in my chest as I headed his way. My feelings for Connor hadn't gone away.

He looked up, stopping me in my tracks.

Our eyes connected.

"Angie." He set the can of corn back on the shelf and turned full-body. He walked over to me and asked, "How have you been?"

"I'm *fine*." I wanted to speak more. I wanted to tell him I cared about him a lot, even more than before, but I couldn't. My words struggled against the fact that I was returning to Tampa in just two days. It wasn't fair to him. There was a sensation around my neck as if a rope was tied around it and someone or something wouldn't let me speak another word.

"Oh." He adjusted his footing. "Well, I'll see you in a little bit over at the inn."

He turned and went back to the corn. Glancing past him, I saw the checkout lane. I stopped and turned to him. With my heart pounding so hard I could feel it in my ears, I grabbed onto his arm. He turned to me. I took a deep breath and began. "What if I told you that I can't stop thinking about you? Every time I look at my phone, I secretly wish you would have texted or called? And it's not because I'm lonely and it's not because I feel sorry for you, but it's because I

see so much goodness in everything you are."

Stepping closer, I tilted my head and peered into his

eyes. "This started out as just friends, but it became

so much *more*. Tell me this became so much more

for you too."

My heart began pounding. I could feel the beat of it

in the base of my throat. Though he wasn't speaking

a word, he spoke volumes.

He shook his head. "I . . ." He hesitated.

"Yes?"

A moment more passed, and the weird situation

turned awkward. I hurried past him and out of the

aisle to check out. As I stood in line, my eyes

watered, draining all hope from my heart. It took

everything inside me not to collapse right there in

the store in a puddle of my own tears.

As I walked out of the grocery store, a gust of snow blew off a snow bank and into my face. The specs of frozen water felt like razor blades as they bounced off my face in the wind. Squinting as I kept my eyes on Serenah's car, I made my way through the frozen tundra of the parking lot.

Climbing inside, I shut the door.

Quiet surrounded me.

With only the muffled sounds of the whooshing wind and snow outside, I let myself collide into my sadness. Sobbing, I smacked the steering wheel and cried out to God. "What do You want me to do, God? Tell me! Show me! Please!"

Tears ran down my cheeks as my sorrow only deepened into the depths of my soul. My voice quieted as I let out another plea to God. "Help me understand. Let me lean on You for understanding .

. ."

⚜

That evening, Connor never showed up for dinner.
After everyone left for the evening and I took a hot
shower, I decided to stay in my bathrobe and steal
the plate of snowball cookies off the counter that
Serenah had made earlier that day. The plan was
sweets and binge-watching classic romantic
comedies on Netflix until I fell asleep. It sounded
like the perfect way to top off a day that was
dreadful.

As I finished my fifth snowball cookie and my
second movie, a knock came on my room's door.
Glancing over, I saw Serenah peek her head in. "Can
I come in?"

I nodded and swiped a few of the crumbs off my chest as I sat up in the bed.

She came in and quietly shut the door behind her. As she came over to the bed, her eyes found the plate of cookies sitting on the bed. "Wondered where they went."

"I wasn't going to eat them all." Grabbing the plate, I handed it to her. She shook her head and set it back down on the bed. Grabbing one, she proceeded to kick her shoes off and climb into bed next to me, letting out a big breath of air. We sat with our backs up against the headboard, and she glanced over. "Connor?" she asked.

Nodding slowly, I kept my eyes on the TV to help keep the welling tears at bay. "I blew it with him, Serenah."

She shook her head. "Blew it? You were really *that*

into him? Where would you even see it going? You live in Tampa. He lives here."

"I know . . ." Reaching over, I grabbed another cookie. "I just haven't felt the way I do about Connor with anyone else since . . . well, a long time."

Thinking about his interaction with the little boy at the tree lighting ceremony and our time together on our outings we had together, I smiled. "When I'm with him, I'm happy. He brings color to the world, and he cares about people and he . . . he's imperfectly perfect for me."

"You told him how you feel?" Serenah asked, taking another cookie from the plate.

"Yep," I replied curtly. Swinging my fist lightly through the air, I said, "Didn't matter. He just stood there, so I just left."

Serenah rubbed my shoulder as the tears fell down

my cheeks. My heart felt knotted a hundred times over as her hand touched my shoulder. "Angie, if he doesn't want to make it work or try it out, you've gotta move on. You can't make people be with you." She laughed. "Right?"

"True," I replied. Turning to her with red eyes, I shook my head. "It's just hard."

Serenah's eyes watered, and she leaned over to hug me. "I know. You'll be okay. You'll get through this."

She was right. In a couple of days, I'd be returning to my life in Tampa. I had received emails from the landlord throughout my trip detailing what was going on back at home. Even though the apartment building had been demolished due to the structural issues after the fire, the landlord relocated all of the residents to a neighboring building. They even found a few of my personal items and got them all into boxes. Going through the remains should keep my mind off *things* for a while.

"I know I'll be okay." Wiping my eyes, I nodded and forced a smile. Glancing at the cookies, I took another. We both laughed.

CHAPTER 14

Somewhere between the snowball cookies, tears and laughter with Serenah last night, I found hope— hope for better days and hope for new beginnings when I returned home to Tampa. It was Christmas morning, and the fact that I wasn't a child with a pile of Christmas gifts under the tree kept me in bed a little bit longer. I prayed, I wept, and I watched the snow fall outside my window.

When I finally rolled out from underneath the covers, it was just shy of ten o'clock. Running my fingers through my hair, I shook the mess enough to make it at least lie down. Opening the door of my room, I found one of the cute stockings Serenah and I had made hanging on the doorknob. Smiling, I loosened it and glanced inside—lip gloss, an assortment of candy, and a Barbie. I laughed. *A Barbie?* Glancing toward the stairs that led upstairs, I shook my head as I narrowed my gaze.

Picking up the tempo of my steps, I headed upstairs and into the living room. Charlie, Serenah and Emma were all up and drinking coffee around the crackling fire in the fireplace. They all looked up at me as I pulled out the Barbie.

"Really?" I asked.

Serenah elbowed Charlie and she laughed as she folded over. "That was *all* Charlie's idea."

"Speaking of," Charlie said, glancing toward the kitchen, "Your Ken doll called. I let it go to message. You can listen to it on the machine in the kitchen."

I thought, *Connor? But why the house phone?*

Heading into the kitchen, I neglected coffee and went straight to the answering machine. Serenah came in as the machine read the date and time. Glancing over at her, I saw she wanted to say something. "*What?*"

"It's *not* Connor." Coming up beside me, she rubbed my back as my shoulders slumped over and confusion whirled about in my mind.

The machine started the message. "Hey, it's me, Peter. You never gave me your number, so I just called the inn . . ." He was already becoming more annoying than Hank Chessler, the kid in the eighth grade who followed me around at lunch and every recess proposing to me for a week straight. I continued listening to the message. "I'm being given an award tonight, and I'd love for you to be there. I know it's strange to have something like this be on

Christmas, but I didn't organize it. I figure this can

be your Christmas gift from me. You could hear

about the work I have been doing, and it could give

us a second chance to get to know each other."

Delete.

Shaking my head as I scoffed, I crossed my arms as I

heard Charlie go out the front door. "How could he

be so selfish and do that? Does he really only think

about himself?"

Serenah caressed my arm and frowned, shaking her

head. "Let me get you a cup of coffee." She went over

to the cupboard, and my eyes followed her

movements as she grabbed a mug and came back

across the kitchen to the coffee pot.

Taking the cup after she poured it, I took a sip as I

heard the door again. Charlie walked into the

kitchen and looked at Serenah and then over to me. "Where's Connor?"

"What?" I replied, setting my cup down. "He wasn't here."

"Yeah, he was. I let him inside, and he went through the—"

Barefoot and in pajamas, I darted through the foyer and out the front door. I saw him with a gift in hand, and he was going back out to his car. "Connor!" I called out as I hurried through the icy cold slush. He stopped as I caught up to him. "What are you doing? You didn't even say 'hi' when you came inside."

Shaking his head as tears streamed down his cheeks, he said, "I heard you perfectly clear in there, Angie."

"Heard what?" My hands spread out as I did not understand what he was talking about.

"I went out of my way to tell you something private,

something intimate, and it was very difficult to—"

He shook his head. "I thought you understood, but

you don't. You just think I'm selfish, that I only

think about myself just like I thought you would."

Tossing the neatly wrapped box toward me, he

sarcastically retorted, "Here, I got you something.

You're right, I shouldn't have." Getting inside his

car, he slammed the door shut and put the car in

reverse. As he pulled out and left, Serenah arrived in

a pair of boots and with a confused look on her face.

Then it clicked. Connor had walked in when we

were talking about the self-centered Peter.

"What happened?" she asked, glancing past me.

"He heard me talking about Peter being selfish and

thought I meant—"

Serenah covered her mouth. "No . . . did you

explain?"

I shook my head. "He didn't even give me a chance. It makes sense though . . . he was pretty nervous about telling me about it." I looked down at the box in my hands when I saw Serenah notice it. She started saying words, but I quieted them out of my mind. I felt like I had been caught up in some kind of stupid soap opera episode I couldn't get out of. *Why did Connor have to walk in at that exact moment when I was rehashing how much I didn't like Peter?* Maybe I needed to stop trying to make something work with this guy. Reminding myself of my early departure tomorrow morning helped cultivate the fact that it needed to be over. We were just two people who liked each other for a moment in time and it just didn't work out. Life would go on even if we didn't end up together.

Snapping out of my thoughts, I remembered the gift

I had in my hand and opened it to find a heart-shaped pendant necklace. A bit cliché, I thought at first, until I flipped it over and saw coordinates. *What is this?* Pulling out my phone as Serenah made her way up to me in the snow, I typed in the coordinates.

"What is it?" she asked.

Tears welled in my eyes as I looked up at her. "He had the coordinates of where we prayed on the plane inscribed on the back."

"How would he know that?"

"I don't know." My eyes turned to the driveway as a sense of longing came over me. *Why does he have to be such a difficult man?* I wondered.

"Well, that's pretty sweet."

Pursing my lips to form a thin line, I shook my head. "He acted like a child. He didn't even let me try to explain. I'm not going to chase after him, Serenah. I'm going home *tomorrow*." Gift and wrapping in hand, I trekked back through the snow toward the inn.

"But Angie . . ." Serenah said as she followed behind me.

Stopping inside the doorway, I turned around as Serenah shut the door. "I don't have time for this kind of thing." Looking over at the fireplace that sat between the foyer and the living room, I shook my head. "I'm an adult woman, and I have a life and business in Tampa." Turning back inside, I headed downstairs to pack my bags.

My cab was set to arrive early the next morning

before the sun even came up, so I woke up a bit

earlier to get a cup of coffee and a jumpstart on the

day. I packed the ornament, but I kept the necklace

and wore it. Though I had decided to press on with

my life, I wouldn't forget Connor. He was the man

who made me realize I could have feelings for

someone after Ted. As I stood in the kitchen

drinking my cup of coffee that morning, I had an

unexpected visitor come waltzing in—Emma.

Smiling, I said, "You just love waking up at night,

don't you?"

"It's morning now," Emma replied with a grin. "I

overheard what happened out front. You didn't talk

to Connor anymore yesterday?"

Shaking my head after my sip of coffee, I set the mug

down on the counter. "He didn't call, and I'm not

going after him. It's stupid. The guy is a little on the

immature side."

Emma began laughing so hard she had to wipe her eyes.

Taken aback, I tilted my head. "What's so funny?"

Emma rested a hand on the counter and shook her head as she wiped a stray tear from the laughter. "What man do you know who isn't immature to some degree?"

I thought of Ted for a moment, and Emma shook her head as if she could read my thoughts.

"Don't try to say *Ted*. Yes, you love him and the memory of him, but don't put him on some kind of pedestal. Men are little boys trapped in a man's body sometimes, Angie. That's just the way they are. We women aren't perfect either. Don't get me wrong."

Hearing the cab arrive outside and honk, I turned toward the doorway that led into the foyer from the kitchen. "That is true, but I'm leaving. I have to get back to my life in Tampa." Leaning over, I grabbed the handle of my suitcase and wheeled it over to her. Wrapping my arms around Emma, I said, "Thank you for the talks and everything. It's been nice getting to know you."

Smiling as we released, she nodded. "I'll be sure to say 'hi' to Ted for you."

Morbid, but true. I grabbed back onto the handle of the suitcase and looked at her. I laughed. "Thank you."

Walking out of the kitchen, I went into the foyer and opened the front door. Through the twilight of the early morning, I could see the headlights of the cab in the driveway. Wheeling my suitcase out, I got in and left.

CHAPTER 15

"Zone one is now ready to board," a young woman's voice echoed through the terminal. Picking up my purse, I saw the corner of my screen light up. Reaching in, I looked to see who was calling. It was Serenah. *What is she calling me for? And at six in the morning?* A twist of worry began to spread outward from the center of my chest.

Walking away from the airport gate, I called her back.

"Serenah?" I said before giving her a chance to

speak.

Cries poured from the other end of the phone, causing me to blanch. Worry soon overtook my entire body, and I darted for the row of seats nearby. "Emma . . ."

Weeping followed the next few minutes.

"I'm leaving the airport now. I'll be there shortly," I said, standing up from the seat and grabbing my suitcase.

"Charlie's a wreck. So am I. You don't have to do that, Angie."

My heart broke for Serenah and for Charlie. Swallowing the smooth pebble-sized knot that I felt form in my throat, I said, "I know I don't *have* to. I want to. We talked about being there for each other, and I'm going to be there for you this time."

Serenah cried. "Okay." Her gentle words dripped with a familiar pain. We said our goodbyes, and I caught the first taxi back to the *Inn at the Lake*.

Somber faces filled the inn as friends and family funneled in and out the next couple of days. Never had I seen so many people pay respects for one woman, one person, one soul. Many of the people who came by were individuals that Charlie and Serenah had never met before that day, people whose lives had somehow been impacted by Emma.

On the third day, Connor showed up.

He was dressed in black slacks and jacket with a

white shirt. His hair was neatly done and his face weighed with sorrow. My heart couldn't help but beat a little harder with him in the room.

After he spoke with Charlie and Serenah, he came over to me as I stood by the windows looking at the lake. His voice was gentle, his touch against my arm welcoming. "Hey . . ." His words rolled off his tongue like I had been the one to lose someone close. It was sweet. He was being sensitive. Though I was upset with him, I was glad he walked over to me.

Turning to him, I raised my brows. "Hey." I didn't have much to say to him. He was not the reason I stayed. Yes, I thought about him after I came back to the inn, but it was an afterthought. It wasn't *the* reason. Spending any more energy and words on him didn't interest me right then. I didn't want to give off the impression to anyone that my motives for staying back at the inn for a bit longer had anything to do with Connor.

"Can we talk?" he asked.

"This isn't the time nor the place, Connor." My tone was sharp and dismissive, but I kept the gentleness that showed respect to Serenah and Charlie in their home. My eyes found Charlie and Serenah talking with an older couple. Seeing Serenah's smile on her face pained me. I knew she was faking it. When everybody was gone, then she'd get real.

Real like she had been for the last few days.

In the spots of time between visitors, Serenah was sneaking off to her private quarters. I followed once. Peeking around the corner of the hallway that led back there, I saw her. There, in front of her steps that led to the bedroom beyond the living room.

On her knees.

Praying.

That woman was an inspiration to me with the grace, the poise and the absolute brilliance in the way she kept connected with God. She contributed all of it to Emma's teaching. Connor adjusted his footing, disrupting my thoughts.

"If you get a moment in the next day or two, give me a call. I'm flying out to New Zealand in two days and would like to talk to you."

Serenah's eyes connected with mine. I saw them glistening, and she needed her cousin, her friend, to help.

"Okay," I replied to Connor and headed across the floor of the living room.

Tending to Serenah and the guests, I began talking to them about my brief conversation with Emma the morning that she had passed. Serenah took the out and retreated. I knew some looked down on her for doing it. I didn't. Jesus retreated all the time from the crowds. It's God first, not others.

Seeing Connor leave, I felt a twinge of sadness creep over me as I glanced his way.

CHAPTER 16

The morning following the funeral, I became

anxious at the thought of Connor flying out to New

Zealand. Maybe it was what Charlie had said about

how you never know how much time is left, as he

stood by Emma's casket at the front of the church.

Sitting on the couch upstairs, I rubbed the corner of

the heart-shaped pendant he had given me,

contemplating calling him. *I'm leaving though . . .*

Serenah came into the living room and I sat up,

swinging my legs over the cushion to sit up straight.

She sat down. Glancing over at me, she forced a

smile.

"How's it going?" I asked.

Serenah's eyes turned toward the fireplace. She must have been formulating some way of answering it as she hesitated for a moment. She shrugged. "I don't know. The phone calls I loathed are slowing, and now, I'm starting to miss them."

Reaching over, I hugged her and she let herself fall into my shoulder. Rubbing her back, it felt as if I could feel every ounce of pain. Loss was something I felt I was an expert in.

Charlie came into the living room from the kitchen a short time later. Serenah and he left to go into Spokane. They were going to grab a bite to eat with a friend of Emma's.

I decided to call Connor.

"Angela," he said, answering in a smooth voice I

found comforting.

"You said you wanted to talk?" I asked.

"Mind if I come over really quickly? My plane doesn't leave till tonight."

Letting out a sigh, I shook my head. Tears and my emotions rattled in my core. "I'm flying out in the morning at six. I'm tired, and I've already had an emotionally draining week. I just didn't want you to think I wouldn't call when you asked me to. Can we just go on living our lives?"

"Sure. If that's what you want, Angie."

"I do."

Hanging up with Connor, I felt an ounce of regret, but then I reminded myself that life would go on without Connor. It did after Ted, and Ted was the love of my life. This, too, would pass.

CHAPTER 17

"Zone one is now ready to board," a young woman's voice chimed. Standing, I grabbed my purse and suitcase to board my plane. As I waited in line, I checked my phone out of curiosity if someone had called. I kind of hoped a special someone would. Clearing my mind, I lifted my chin high and looked forward in line.

In my seat on the plane, I began making mental bullet points of what I'd do once I returned home. Go through all the burned up leftovers of my old life and replace the furniture with the insurance money. *Maybe I'll get a job.* My time at the tree lot made for certain I'd never do that job again, but working back at the soap factory like the good ole' days wouldn't be so bad. Yeah, something to fill the time. At least a few days a week.

Knock, knock

Startled, I lifted my head from my relaxed position of my seat and looked out my little window beside me.

"Connor?" My eyes widened and my heart cleaved against my ribcage. "What are you doing?" I shouted as I jumped out of my seat, landing almost in the man's lap beside me. I knocked the man's newspaper into his lap, and he grumbled. I jolted back to the window and Connor. My heart was racing as I shouted as close as I could to the window, "What are you doing here?" I repeated.

Muffled, but still understandable, Connor spoke. "I don't want to just 'go on living my life'." My heart fluttered, and then something distracted him from below. His eyebrows shot up.

"What is all the commotion about?" a flight attendant asked, leaning into the row to see out the window. Her eyes widened as she saw him and quickly made her way back toward the front of the plane, alerted the pilot, and called security.

I turned back to the window, and Connor was gone. Pushing my face up against the window, I tried to see below and I couldn't. My heart began pounding, and I got up out of my seat, grabbed my purse, and headed for the exit. Stopping at the flight attendants, I asked, "Excuse me. What is going to happen to that man?"

The flight attendant turned to me and said, "He'll probably go to jail. You can't just be on runways in this day and age. Security got him."

Hurrying, I maneuvered through the people trying to get on the plane and headed back into the airport to go find him.

Lips pursed, back straight, and my phone dead, I waited for Airport Security to release Connor. He had been in there for close to three hours now, and I was becoming increasingly worried about what would happen to him.

He was finally released.

The gray door opened and he came waltzing into the room. He didn't seem to have a bit of remorse. He was all smiles. Standing up, I went over to him and we hugged. His embrace was warm, perfect, sublime. I was worried about him for hours. I thought they'd water board him, maybe throw him in a federal prison. Those ideas came to me an hour into waiting when I saw two federal agents arrive and go into the room, causing my imagination to take off running.

Releasing from our embrace, he tilted his head and his eyes bounced between both of mine. "I was stupid, Angela. *Really* stupid. I know we can probably go on living our lives and whatever, but I was about to go to New Zealand yesterday, and I realized I don't want to."

He gently touched my hands, holding them in his. "I

could go on, but my heart cannot. I feel alive when I'm with you, Angela. Even when I'm just in the same vicinity as you, I feel better, like my heart is beating for the first time. You make me want to be a better person. I got you that necklace with the coordinates of where we prayed because through that storm, we had a moment—a moment that blossomed into something beautiful, Angela. I believe God uses the storms we go through in life to not only bring people closer together with each other, but closer to Him. I *love* you."

Tears welled in my eyes as I felt his words touch my soul. He looked like he was about to say more, but I stopped him. "I love you too, Connor." Leaning up onto my toes, I kissed him.

Relaxing his shoulders, he pulled me in and we continued to kiss.

"Hey," the security guard at the desk interrupted. "Can you not?"

We both laughed, and Connor put his arm around my shoulders as we started walking through the airport.

"What did security say? What's going to happen to you?"

"I'm getting a *huge* fine and will probably have to go to court."

Stopping, I gently grabbed his arm to stop him. "Why aren't you upset about it? That seems *really* bad. How did you even get up there?"

A grin snuck in from the corner of his lips. "I tried to call you, and when I didn't get an answer, I hijacked the luggage lift. I had to get to you. As for being upset, I got the girl. How could I be upset?"

Pulling him close to me, I leaned on my toes and kissed him. He wrapped his arms around me and smoothed my hair with his hand.

From that point on, Connor and I would be together. After finding a place for breakfast that morning, we mapped out a plan to get me relocated to Spokane. I didn't have to, but I sold my shares to Robert after I broke the news to him and found out he had been interested in buying them ever since Ted had passed.

I hated flying, but I'm glad I had that Monday morning in November. It was through One Monday Prayer that I'd found Connor.

The End.

Did you enjoy the Book?

Please
Leave a Review

BOOK PREVIEW

Preview of "Amongst the Flames"

Prologue

Fire. Four letters, two vowels and one reaction.

That reaction depends on who you are. For me and the fellas at Station 9 in downtown Spokane, our reaction is one of quickness, speed and precision. A few seconds delay could mean someone's life. We don't have time to think, only do. And we don't do this for the recognition or because it's just some job, we do it because this is what we were born to do. My resume, if I had one, would only say one thing on it: Firefighter. I'm one of those guys that you don't really think about unless something has gone terribly wrong. Usually it's when your house is on fire.

I won't bore you with the countless calls where we just show up with our lights on and we're just there to support the police and ambulance. I'm sure you've seen us sitting across the street quietly once or twice while they wheel Mrs. Johnson out on a gurney to the ambulance at three o'clock in the morning. I also won't explain to you the hundred calls a year we get on burning popcorn in a kitchen. No. This story I'm going to share with you is not only about the worst fire I had ever seen in my life, but it'll also encompass how important God is, not only in marriage, but in life.

This is not a story you'll find on the front page of your local newspaper while you're sipping your morning cup of coffee. You also won't catch it on the ten o'clock news. Nope. Instead, it's a story that will inspire you to look at life differently and challenge you to believe that with God even the worst fire you face is nothing in comparison with His power, grace and mercy.

Belief in God is not really an option for me when I run into burning buildings to save lives. It's a core fundamental building block of who I am. I won't sit here and tell you that I'm a perfect Christian though; that would be a lie. Soon enough, you'll read about my plethora of issues and flaws amongst the pages that follow. What I will do is stay true to the truth the best that I can. I'm not telling this story to make a record of my sins or those of others. I'm giving you this story to give you hope. Hope of a brighter tomorrow that you can look forward to, hope of a world where acceptance isn't only preached, but it's applied alongside the scriptures to our lives.

I am Cole Taylor and this is my story.

Chapter 1

Walking down an aisle in the grocery store with

Kane, Micah and Greg one morning at about eight

o'clock I couldn't help but laugh a little. I caught

Kane checking out a pretty brunette a few aisles over

in the bakery.

"Always on the prowl, aren't ya?" I asked, smiling

over at him. Kane was the station's notorious single

twenty-three-year-old male with nothing but

women on his mind. He once admitted to me that

he bought a full set of turnouts online from an ex-

fireman just so he could suit up in a full fireman

outfit for a girl.

"She's cute," Kane replied with a half-grin on his

face. He shot another look over at her and his smile

grew.

"Maybe she can bake you a cake or something?" Greg said with a soft but sarcastic tone as he grabbed a box of pasta from the shelf. Greg was one of the quieter guys on the crew.

Micah and I erupted in laughter. Kane smiled and said, "I'm sure there's more to her than that."

"How would you even know that?" I asked.

He shrugged. "It's a hunch, I know about these things."

"Well, at least you know she has a sweet side," Micah added. Kane laughed a little as he pushed the cart down towards the end of the aisle.

On the way over to the meat section of the store, a man with furrowed eyebrows made a beeline for us. Leaning into Kane's ear, I said, "Move the cart out of his way." Kane did, but it didn't help. The elderly gentleman shifted his footing to line up with our

cart as he continued towards us.

Arriving at us, the man latched his worn hands to

each side of our cart and demanded in a sharp tone,

"What are you doing here?"

"Same as most people here, just grocery shopping...

you?" Kane asked, crossing his arms as he released

his grip from the cart.

"Are you on the clock right now?" the man asked. He

shot a quick look at each of us individually as if we

were caught in some kind of predicament.

"Yeah," I replied, stepping in front of Kane and up to

the gentleman. I knew I needed to get between them

before Kane did something stupid. His fuse was

short when it came to people who didn't respect

firefighters. For instance, there was a call one time

that Kane and I were on where the man whose

house was on fire started complaining to us about how long it took us to respond. Kane took his revenge inside the home when he used the butt of his axe to smash the guy's big screen TV.

"Is there a problem going on in the store we should know about?" Micah asked, looking over my shoulder at the man. Micah was my best friend at the station and he was always looking for the best in people no matter what the situation appeared to be.

"Yeah, matter of fact there is a problem ya chump! And I'm looking right at it," he shouted, raising his hands from the cart. I looked back at Kane as I knew the comment would set him off. Catching his gaze before he said anything, I could see Kane trying to keep his mouth shut. That little stunt he pulled at that fire by smashing the guy's TV landed him with a suspension without pay.

Micah raised his hands. "We're just trying to get to some supplies, Sir."

"Yeah– he's right. We don't want any trouble, Sir. We need to keep moving." I grabbed onto the cart and began walking past the disgruntled citizen.

"This is how my tax dollars is spent, huh?" He asked as he laughed sarcastically, shaking his head at us.

"I'm filing a complaint with your station!" he said from behind us. He must have been looking at the back of our fleece pullovers as he continued,

"Station 9... Who's in charge over there?"

"Thomas Sherwood and Sean Hinley are our Captains and Paul Jensen's the Chief," I said over my shoulder to him.

"I'll be calling them right away!" he shouted.

We all three managed to keep our cool and made it over to the meats. As we came up to the bunker with steaks and stopped, Kane said, "We risk our lives, yet people still find a reason to complain... What is with that?" He glanced back at the angry man as he now appeared to be arguing with a grocery store worker.

I turned to Kane. "Do you do this job because you want people to think you're a hero?"

"No..." he replied softly. "But that kind of thing just isn't right."

"No, it's not right," I agreed. "But we don't do this to impress people, Kane. You know that. We do this job because it's our duty and we do it to protect the people of Spokane. We serve them, no matter how poorly we get treated."

"Cole's right, man," Micah said with a nod. "We can't let people like him get in our head."

"We can't let them undermine our reasons for doing

this," Greg added.

"I find honor in what we do and someone like that just bugs me."

"I know it does," I replied, putting a hand on his shoulder. "And thank you for not saying anything to him." I turned back to the steaks. "What cut do we want boys?" I asked.

Suddenly dispatch came over all our radios for a fire at the Canyon Creek Apartments on South Westcliff. We all four began sprinting for the front doors. My heart began pounding as adrenaline coursed through every one of my veins. Weaving between the aisles and shopping carts, we made our way outside. Spotting a cart boy on the way through the parking lot, I stopped and told him about our cart in the back of the store. He thanked me and I headed over to the truck.

Micah jumped into the driver seat. He was the ladder company's engineer and that meant the man behind the wheel. Greg sat up front with Micah; his role varied and depended much on what was needed on each call. Kane and I were the guys who did search and rescue, cut power and helped with ventilation cuts on the roof.

As Kane and I suited up in the back, Kane asked, "Did you see that chick in the bakery look concerned as we dashed out of there?"

I laughed. "No, didn't catch that," I said, pulling up my suspenders across the front of my chest.

"When we go back later I'm going to go talk to her. Bet I can get those digits," he replied as he slid his Nomax head and neck protector over his eyes. "I'll for sure get her number."

"She could be married," I replied.

"Nah, I saw her left hand when she was putting out donuts in the window earlier."

I laughed. "Wait... what ever happened to that Heidi girl? I almost completely forgot about her."

"He got bored of her," Micah said over his shoulder to us. "He can't seem to stay interested in one gal; you know that."

"Shouldn't you be keeping your eyes on the road?" Kane retorted.

"Really though, man, what happened?" I asked, looking over at Kane.

"Just didn't work out," Kane said as he shrugged.

We slowed down as we arrived at the scene. Glancing out my window, I could see the fire had already engulfed much of the apartment complex and I felt another surge of adrenaline. I was excited and yet terrified out of my mind of the unknown that lay before me. It was that way every time we got a call.

Glancing at the other fire truck on scene, I saw Thomas Sherwood, the shift captain of station 9 and my father-in-law. He was already on scene along with the other guys who rode over on the engine truck. They were already about done hooking up the hose to the hydrant as we came to a complete stop. Leaping from my seat, my feet barely hit the pavement before the captain reached me.

"We need a grab on the second floor," he shouted. "There's a four year old girl in apartment one-forty-two." My heart felt like it skipped a beat as I looked up at the roaring flames. Saving lives wasn't anything new for me, but I never could get used to it. Even after ten years of service, every time lives were at stake, it was difficult, especially when the lives of children were involved.

"Got it," I replied as I grabbed my oxygen tank from the side of the truck and secured it onto my back. Grabbing my axe and Halligan bar, I turned as I pulled my mask over my face and put on my helmet. A hand on my shoulder stopped me from heading directly to the building.

"And, Cole," the captain said as I turned around.

"Yeah?" I asked.

"Be careful in there, I don't have the energy to explain to my daughter how her husband died today."

"No worries, you haven't had to yet," I replied. Turning, I looked at the apartment entrance and saw the black smoke billowing out the front door. I jogged up to the door and as I entered, I saw Rick, starting the exterior attack on the fire from outside with his hose in hand. He was spraying down the nearby building so it would not catch on fire. I gave him a nod. Rick Alderman was one of the veterans on the crew. It was he, Micah and I for the past ten years at fire station 9. Kane came on a couple years after me and the others all were fairly new, each under five years. The older vets from the old days when I first started —like Hillman and Conrad— moved away and transferred to other stations. But no matter who came or went, when we were on the scene we were like that of a brotherhood. No man left behind, ever.

Coming inside the burning building, I immediately noticed the extreme temperatures inside. It wasn't typical, a bit warmer than I was used to. I pushed the sensation of being trapped in a furnace out of my mind as I ventured in further. I trekked through the black smoke and up the stairs in search for the child. My jacket was failing to keep the high temperatures of the heat from my skin and the burning was digging in. Ignoring common-sense reactions to extreme situations is a requirement that they don't advertise in the job description. Who in his right mind after all would run into a burning building, on purpose?

My visibility was low at the top of the stairs inside. The charcoal-black smoke was thick and filled every square inch. Seeing a door within reach, I came up to it. Squinting, I could see it read 'one forty four.' It wasn't the one I needed. I trudged through the ever-thickening smoke as the heat gnawed at my skin until I found the apartment I needed. One-forty-two. Relieved, I grabbed for the door knob, but found it locked. Taking a few steps back, I launched a kick to the door that would have impressed an MMA fighter, but it wasn't enough to make it budge. I brought my Halligan front side and stuck it right between the door and the frame. My skin continued to burn from the heat and my muscles screamed in pain as I pried open the door. Finally, it budged open.

Stepping through the smoke filled room, I shouted, "Fire department, Call out!" The sound of the roaring flames and falling pieces of debris made it nearly impossible to hear anything else.

Lowering myself to the floor, I moved through the living room and reached a doorway. An explosion suddenly came from another part of the building. Covering my helmet, I braced myself for any falling debris. Continuing through the doorway and smoke, I noticed a smoldering teddy bear next to me. This must be the girl's room, I thought to myself as I raised my head to survey the room. Trying to see through the smoke was difficult, but I spotted a closet across the floor. I repeated, "Fire department, Call out!" as I inched my way over to the closet. Getting to the closet, I found the little girl almost about to lose consciousness. Ripping my mask off in a frenzy, I shoved it over her face and said, "It is going to be okay, I'm going to get you out of here." She struggled to breathe into the mask. Our breathing apparatuses weren't so easy to use when not properly trained. "Just try to take small and short breaths," I said.

I grabbed the little girl and held her close to my chest in my arms, using myself as a shield as I crawled back towards the doorway. Once back into the living room, I stood up for the rest of the journey out. But before I could reach the front door of the apartment, an explosion came from the kitchen. Covering the girl as much as possible and dropping to the floor, I protected her from the blast. But a piece of metal shot across the room from the explosion and hit me in the upper arm. I thanked God it was only my arm as I regained my footing and continued to the door with the girl. My adrenaline was pumping and my heart was pounding so hard that I had no idea how bad my wound was. As I came to the stairs that led out of the apartment, pain suddenly shot through my arm, sending me collapsing to the top of the stairs.

Lying there I turned my head and looked down to the base of the stairs. I could see through the mostly faded smoke as Kane came rushing through the doorway and up the stairs to me.

Did you enjoy this sample? Go to

www.tkchapin.com and get a copy today!

BOOK PREVIEW

Preview of "The Perfect Cast"

Prologue

Each of us has moments of impact in life. Sometimes it's in the form of *love*, and sometimes in the form of *sadness*. It is in these times that our world changes forever. They shape us, they define us, and they transform us from the people we once were into the people we now are.

The summer before my senior year of high school is one that will live with me forever. My parents' relationship was on the rocks, my brother was more annoying than ever, and I was forced to leave the world I loved and cared about in Seattle. A summer of change, a summer of growth, and a summer I'll never forget.

Chapter 1 ~ Jess

Jess leaned her head against the passenger side window as she stared out into the endless fields of wheat and corn. She felt like an alien in a foreign land, as it looked nothing like the comfort of her home back in Seattle.

She was convinced her friends were lucky to not have a mother who insisted on whisking them away to spend the *entirety* of their summer out in the middle of nowhere in Eastern Washington. She would have been fine with a weekend visit, but the entire summer at Grandpa's? That was a bit uncalled for, and downright wrong. Her mother said the trip was so Jess and her brother Henry could spend time with her grandpa Roy, but Jess had no interest in doing any such thing.

On the car ride to Grandpa's farm to be dropped off and abandoned, Jess became increasingly annoyed with her mother. Continually, her mother would glance over at Jess, looking for conversation. Ignoring her mom's attempts to make eye contact with her, Jess kept her eyes locked and staring out the window. Every minute, and every second of the car ride, Jess spent wishing the summer away.

After her mother took the exit off the freeway that led out to the farm, a loud pop came from the driver side tire and brought the car to a grinding halt. Her mom was flustered, and quickly got out of the car to investigate the damage. Henry, Jess's obnoxious and know-it-all ten-year-old brother, leaned between the seats and glanced out the windshield at their mom.

"Stop being so annoying," Jess said, pushing his face back between the seats. He sat back and then began to reach for the door. Jess looked back at him and asked, "What are you doing?"

"I'm going to help Mom."

"Ha. You can't help her; you don't know how to change a tire."

"Well, I am going to *try*." Henry climbed out of the car and shut it forcefully. Jess didn't want this summer to exist and it hadn't even yet begun. If only she could fast forward, and her senior year of high school could start, she'd be happy. But that wasn't the case; there was no remote control for her life. Instead, the next two and half months were going to consist of being stuck out on a smelly farm with Henry and her grandpa. She couldn't stand more than a few minutes with her brother, and being stuck in a house with no cable and *him*? That was a surefire sign that one of them wasn't making it home alive. Watching her mother stare blankly at the car, unsure of what to do, Jess laughed a little to herself. *If you wouldn't have left Dad, you would have avoided this predicament.* Her dad knew how to fix everything. Whether it was a flat tire, a problematic science project or her fishing pole, her dad was always there for her no matter what. That was up until her mother walked out on him, and screwed everybody's life up. He left out of the country on a three month hiatus. Jess figured he had a broken heart and just needed the time away to process her mom leaving him in the dust.

Henry stood outside the car next to his mother, looking intently at the tire. Accidentally catching eye contact with her mother, Jess rolled her eyes. Henry had been trying to take over as the *man of the house* ever since the split. It was cute at first, even to Jess, but his rule of male superiority became rather old quickly when Henry began telling Jess not to speak to her mother harshly and to pick up her dirty laundry. Taking the opportunity to cut into her mom, Jess rolled down her window. "Why don't you call Grandpa? Oh, that's right... he's probably outside and doesn't have a cell phone... but even if he did, he wouldn't have reception."

"Don't start with me, Jess." Her mother scowled at her. Jess watched as her mother turned away from the car and spotted a rickety, broken down general store just up the road.

Her mom began to walk along the side of the road with Henry. Jess didn't care that she wasn't invited on the family trek along the road. It was far too hot to walk anywhere, plus she preferred the coolness of the air conditioning. She wanted to enjoy the small luxury of air conditioning before getting to her grandpa's, where she knew there was sure to be nothing outside of box fans.

Jess pulled her pair of ear buds out from the front pouch of her backpack and plugged them into her phone. Tapping into her music as she put the ear buds in, she set the playlist to shuffle. Staring back out her window, she noticed a cow feeding on a pile of hay through the pine trees, just over the other side of a barbed wire fence. *I really am in the middle of nowhere.*

Chapter 2 ~ Roy

The blistering hot June sun shone brightly through the upper side of the barn and through the loft's open doorway, illuminating the dust and alfalfa particles that were floating around in the air. Sitting on a hay bale in the upper loft of the barn, Roy watched as his nineteen-year-old farmhand Levi retrieved each bale of hay from the conveyor that sat at the loft's doorway. Each bale of alfalfa weighed roughly ninety pounds; it was a bit heavier than the rest of the grass hay bales that were stored in the barn that year. Roy enjoyed watching his farmhand work. He felt that if he watched him enough, he might be able to rekindle some of the strength that he used to have in his youth.

While Roy was merely watching, that didn't

protect him from the loft's warmth, and sweat quickly began to bead on his forehead. Reaching for his handkerchief from his back pocket, he brought it to his forehead and dabbed the sweat. Roy appreciated the help of Levi for the past year. Whether it was feeding and watering the cattle, fixing fences out in the fields, or shooting the coyotes that would come down from the hill and attack the cows, Levi was always there and always helping. He was the son of Floyd Nortaggen, the man who ran the dairy farm just a few miles up the road. If it wasn't for Levi, Roy suspected he would have been forced to give up his farm and move into a retirement home. Roy knew retirement homes were places where people went to die, and he just wasn't ready to die. And he didn't want to die in a building full of people that he didn't know; he wanted to die out on his farm, where he always felt he belonged.

"Before too long, I'll need you to get up on the roof and get those shingles replaced. I'm afraid one good storm coming through this summer could ruin the hay."

Levi glanced up at the roof as he sat on the final bale of hay he had stacked. Wiping away the sweat from his brow with his sleeve, he looked over to Roy. "I'm sure I could do that. How old are the shingles?"

A deep smile set into Roy's face as he thought about when he and his father had built the barn back when he was just a boy. "It's been forty years now." His father had always taken a fancy to his older brother, but when his brother had gone away on a mission trip for the summer, his dad had relied on Roy for help with constructing the barn. Delighted, he'd spent the summer toiling in the heat with his dad. He helped lay the foundation, paint the barn and even helped put on the roof. Through sharing the heat of summer and sips of lemonade that his mother would bring out to them, Roy and his father grew close, and remained that way until his father's death later in life.

"Forty years is a while... my dad re-shingled his barn after twenty."

"Shingles usually last between twenty and thirty years." Roy paused to let out a short laugh. "I've been pushing it for ten. Really should have done it last summer when I first started seeing the leaks, but I hadn't the strength and was still too stubborn to accept your help around here."

"I imagine it's quite difficult to admit needing help. I don't envy growing old –no offense."

"None taken," Roy replied, glancing over his shoulder at the sound of a car coming up the driveway over the bridge. "I believe my grandchildren have arrived."

"I'll be on my way then; I don't want to keep you, and it seems to me we are done here."

"Thank you for the help today. I'll write your check, but first get the hay conveyor equipment put away. Just come inside the farmhouse when you're done."

Roy climbed down the ladder and Levi followed behind him. As Roy exited the barn doors, he could see his daughter faintly behind the reflection of the sun off the windshield of her silver

Prius. Love overcame him as he made eye contact with her. His daughter was the apple of his eye, and he felt she was the only thing he had done right in all the years of his life on earth. He'd never admit it to anyone out loud, but Tiff was his favorite child. She was the first-born and held a special place in his heart. The other kids gravitated more to their mother anyway; Tiffany and he were always close.

Parking in front of the garage that matched the paint of the barn, red with white trim, His daughter Tiffany stepped out of the driver side door and smiled at him. Hurrying her steps through the gravel, she ran up to her dad and hugged him as she let out what seemed to be a sigh of relief.

Watching over her shoulder as Jess got out of the car, Roy saw her slam the door. He suspected the drive hadn't gone that well for the three of them, but did the courtesy of asking without assuming. "How was the drive?"

"You don't want to ask..." she replied, glancing back at Jess as her daughter lingered near the corner of the garage.

Roy smiled. "I have a fresh batch of lemonade inside," he said, trying to lighten the tension he could sense. Seeing Henry was still in the backseat fiddling with something, Roy went over to one of the back doors and opened the door.

"Hi Grandpa," Henry said, looking up at him.

Leaning his head into the car, Roy smiled. "I'm looking for Henry, have you seen him? Because there's no way you are, Henry! He's just a little guy." Roy used his hand to show how tall Henry *should be* and continued, "About this tall, if my memory serves me correctly."

Henry laughed. "Stop Grandpa! It's me, I'm Henry!"

"I know... I'm just playing with you, kiddo! I haven't seen you in years! You've grown like a weed! Give your ol' Grandpa a hug!" Henry dropped his tablet on the seat and climbed over a suitcase of Jess's to embrace his grandpa in a warm hug.

"Can we go fishing Grandpa? Can we go today?"

Roy laughed as he stood upright. "Maybe tomorrow. The day is going to be over soon and I'd like to visit with your mother some."

Henry dipped his chin to his chest as he sighed. "Okay." Reaching into the back trunk area of the car, Henry grabbed his backpack and then scooted off his seat and out from the car. Just then, Jess let out a screech, which directed everyone's attention over to her at the garage.

"A mouse, are you kidding me?" With a look of disgust, she stomped off around Levi's truck, and down the sidewalk that led up to the farmhouse.

"Aren't you forgetting something?" Tiffany asked, which caused Jess to stop in her tracks. She turned around and put her hand over her brow to shield the sun.

"What, mom?"

"Your suitcases... maybe?" Tiffany replied with a sharp tone.

Roy placed a hand on Tiffany's shoulder. "That's okay. Henry and I can get them."

"No. Jess needs to get them." Roy could tell that his daughter was attempting to draw a line in the sand. A line that Roy and his late wife Lucille had drawn many times with her and the kids.

"Really, Mom?" Jess asked, placing a hand on her hip. "Those suitcases are heavy; the men should carry them. Grandpa is right."

Henry tugged on his mother's shirt corner. "I think you should let this one go, Mother." He smiled and nodded to Roy. "Grandpa and I have it."

Tiffany shook her head and turned away from Jess as she went to the back of the car. "She's so difficult, Dad. I hate it," Tiffany said, slapping the trunk. "She doesn't understand how life really works."

"Winnie," Roy replied. "Pick your battles."

The nickname *Winnie* came from when she was three years old. She would wake up in the middle of the night, push a chair up to the pantry and sneak the honey back into her bedroom. On several occasions, they would awaken the next day to find her snuggling an empty bottle of honey underneath her covers.

"I know. It's just hard sometimes, because everything is a battle with her lately."

Did you enjoy this preview?

*Pick up a copy of **The Perfect Cast** today!*

OTHER BOOKS

Diamond Lake Series

One Thursday Morning (Book 1)

One Friday Afternoon (Book 2)

One Saturday Evening (Book 3)

One Sunday Drive(Book 4)

One Monday Prayer

Embers & Ashes Series

Amongst the Flames (Book 1)

Out of the Ashes (Book 2)

Up in Smoke (Book 3)

After the Fire (Book 4)

Love's Enduring Promise Series

The Perfect Cast (Book 1)

Finding Love (Book 2)

Claire's Hope (Book 3)

Dylan's Faith (Book 4)

Stand Alones

Love Again

Love Interrupted

A Chance at Love

The Lost Truth

Visit www.tkchapin.com for all the latest releases

Subscribe to the Newsletter for special

Prices, free gifts and more!

www.tkchapin.com

ABOUT THE AUTHOR

T.K. CHAPIN writes Christian Romance books designed to inspire and tug on your heart strings. He believes that telling stories of faith, love and family help build the faith of Christians and help non-believers see how God can work in the life of believers. He gives all credit for his writing and storytelling ability to God. The majority of the novels take place in and around Spokane Washington, his hometown. Chapin makes his home in the Pacific Northwest and has the pleasure of raising his daughter with his beautiful wife Crystal. To find out more about T.K. Chapin or his books, visit his website at www.tkchapin.com.

CPSIA information can be obtained
at www.ICGtesting.com
Printed in the USA
LVOW13s1710270218
568057LV00013B/571/P